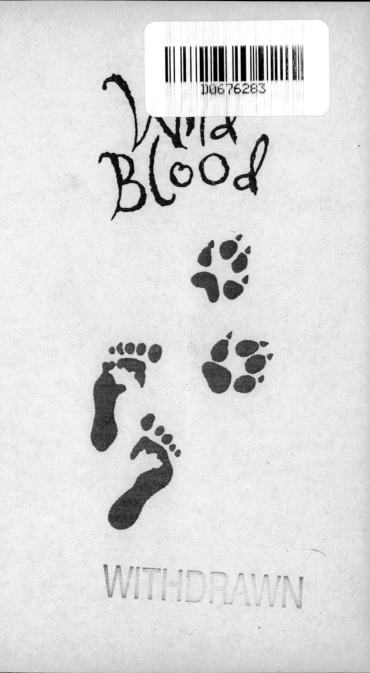

# Wild Blood

*Also by Kate Thompson*

Switchers
Midnight's Choice

# Wild Blood

# KATE THOMPSON

## RED FOX

A Red Fox Book
Published by Random House Children's Books
20 Vauxhall Bridge Road, London SW1V 2SA

A division of The Random House Group Ltd
London Melbourne Sydney Auckland
Johannesburg and agencies throughout the world

Copyright © 1999 Kate Thompson

1 3 5 7 9 10 8 6 4 2

First published in Great Britain by
The Bodley Head Children's Books 1999

Red Fox edition 2000

Printed and bound in Great Britain by
Cox & Wyman Ltd, Reading, Berkshire

Papers used by Random House
are natural, recyclable products made from wood grown in
sustainable forests. The manufacturing processes conform to
the environmental regulations of the country of origin.

The Random House Group Limited Reg. No. 954009
www.randomhouse.co.uk

ISBN 0 09 926628 8

*For Sara Jane*

*I would like to thank The Tyrone Guthrie Centre at Annaghmakerrig, the Ennistymon Library and Jane Tottenham, who have all made work space available to me at crucial times.*

# CHAPTER ONE

When her parents told her their summer plans, Tess waited for the right moment, then turned herself into a swift and flew out over the city to visit her friend Lizzie. Human again, sitting at the old woman's fireside, Tess poured out her troubles.

'They're going on holiday without me!' she said. 'They're sending me to stay with my cousins in Clare. For three weeks!'

'I don't know what you's complaining about,' said Lizzie. 'The country is a great place for children.'

Tess stifled her irritation. 'I'm not a child, Lizzie.'

'Maybe you is and maybe you isn't. But you's still a Switcher, and that's all that matters. You'll have a great time down there in Clare.'

'I'm still a Switcher, all right. But not for much longer. That's why I came to see you. I'm going to have my fifteenth birthday while I'm down there.'

'Hmm.' Lizzie rubbed the chin of the tabby cat on

her lap. 'That is a bit sticky, I suppose.' The cat began to purr like a soft engine.

'There's no way of telling them how important it is, you see,' said Tess.

They fell quiet, each of them mulling over the problem in her own mind. At the dawn of their fifteenth birthdays, all Switchers lose their power to change their shape, and have to decide on what form they'll take for the rest of their lives. Lizzie knew that, because she had been a Switcher in her younger days, but Tess's parents knew nothing of their daughter's powers or her problems.

'Has you decided yet?' asked Lizzie. 'What you'll be?'

Tess shook her head.

'Then maybe it'll be easier for you without them around,' said Lizzie. 'And maybe Clare is the best place you could be.'

'Why?'

'You has wild blood in your veins, Tess. All Switchers has. And you might get a bit of help from your ancestors down that way.'

'My ancestors?'

'Be sure to give them my regards if you happen upon them, you hear?'

'What do you mean, my ancestors?'

The cat on the old woman's lap had been joined by two others, and three different purrs were creating guttural music. Lizzie seemed to be orchestrating it, with a stroke here and a rub there. Tess thought she had nothing more to say, and knew better than to try and push her. But eventually Lizzie looked up. Her sharp old eyes were full of life and humour.

'Does we believe what we sees, eh?' she said. 'Or does we see what we believe?'

# CHAPTER TWO

On her first night in her aunt's country farmhouse, Tess had a strange and frightening dream. In the dream she was in a dark and magical place and she was watching Kevin, who had turned into a rat. Strange beings, huge and vague, hovered in the background, watching them. Tess knew that Kevin was afraid but she didn't know what to do, and a terrible urgency pervaded the dream so that a feeling of terror washed through her, again and again.

The fear woke her and she sat up in the bedroom she shared with one of her cousins. There was a strange, roaring sound which seemed to be coming from all around her, and for a long moment Tess lay frozen, holding her breath. Then, with a flood of relief, she realised what it was. Rain. It was thundering down on to the roof above her head, streaming into the gutters, sloshing away in the down-pipes and the drains. She breathed out.

The dream made no sense. Kevin was well past fifteen and could no longer Switch. Whatever dangers he might encounter in life, becoming a rat again wasn't one of them. Tess snuggled back into the bed and wrapped the covers around her. Gradually the fear receded and the sound of the rain was like music, lulling her back to sleep.

The following morning Tess woke to the sound of the cattle in the field beyond the yard grumbling together as they waited for their breakfast. The rain had stopped. In the other bed, her cousin Orla was still asleep, wheezing slightly with the asthma that had tormented her for most of her eleven years. Although Tess saw her cousins regularly when they visited Dublin, it was many years since she had visited them at their own home, in the wilds of County Clare. The sounds and smells of the countryside were so delightful that she forgot, for the moment, that she didn't want to be there and was still annoyed with her parents for going off on holiday without her. She stretched luxuriously and languished for a few minutes, listening to the birds. Then she got up and went down to help her Uncle Maurice with the milking.

A white cat with sky blue eyes was sitting on top of the oil tank in the yard. It watched Tess closely as she crossed to where her Uncle Maurice was letting out the dogs, Bran and Sceolan. He was surprised to see her.

'You're up early,' he said.

'Can I help?' asked Tess.

'You can, girl, indeed you can.'

He was heading for the feed-shed as he spoke, and Tess followed. But when he opened the door he stood frozen to the spot. Despite his large bulk in the doorway, Tess could see all that she needed to. The floor of the shed was strewn with dairy nuts, spilled from the paper sacks which were stacked against the wall. The smell of rodents was almost overpowering and Tess wasn't at all surprised to see that Bran and Sceolan weren't in any hurry to go in there. Indeed, a moment later they turned tail and fled, as Uncle Maurice's temper erupted.

'Damn and blast those flamin' rats!' he yelled, striding into the shed. As Tess watched, rooted to the spot, he punched feedbags, kicked walls, opened the infiltrated feed-bins and slammed their wooden lids. Even the restless cattle stopped complaining and waited politely, fearful that the violence might be turned upon them. But at last it abated. In silence, Uncle Maurice filled buckets and emptied them into the mangers. In silence, Tess helped. But her uncle's anger still resounded in the slamming of bolts as he opened the door of the milking parlour, and the cattle gave him a wide berth as they came in to take their places.

The sun was climbing high in a cloudless sky by the time the breakfast dishes were washed and put away. Tess asked if she could go out for a walk, and her Aunt Deirdre consented. The two boys, ten-year-old Brian and three-year-old Colm had already gone out to try to catch the bad-tempered little Shetland pony that grazed among the cattle, but for a few awkward moments it seemed likely that Orla was going to tag along as well. To Tess's relief, her aunt wouldn't allow it.

'What would you do if you couldn't catch your breath out there, child? What would poor Tess do?'

Before Orla could appeal the decision, Tess slipped out of the back door and headed off quickly across the broad, green meadows of the farm. She was delighted that she hadn't been made to come up with an excuse for wanting to be alone. It was never easy to lie about it, but it was vital that she had time to herself.

To her annoyance, Sceolan, the younger of the two dogs, attached himself to her heels, and no amount of stern instruction could persuade him to go back. But before they had gone too far he spotted Bran and Uncle Maurice gathering sheep and raced off to make a nuisance of himself. Tess pretended she hadn't seen them and walked on, climbing gates and walls until she came to the end of the clean meadows. The highest of them had been bulldozed in the distant past and the piles of cleared stone made untidy walls. Beyond, the rough land began; the area that Tess couldn't wait to explore.

She looked back at the house. She had already covered a good distance and it was unlikely that anyone was watching, but she could still see Uncle Maurice and hear him swearing at Sceolan, and she felt much too exposed to Switch. So she walked on, over ground that became rockier and more difficult at every step. Beneath her feet the limestone was full of fossils. Here and there huge flakes of it broke away and revealed the shapes of shells or mud patterns; the rock's own memory of its origins, deep beneath some ancient sea. The sense of great age gave the whole place a mysterious air, and a thrill of adventure coursed through Tess's bones.

Ahead of her the land rose gradually for another quarter of a mile, then reared up abruptly in a towering cliff face that her cousins referred to as The

6

Crag. At its foot she could see ash trees stretching out of a forest of hazel; a perfect place to explore and try some of her favourite animal forms, perhaps for the last time. She quickened her pace and before long she had come to the edge of the woods.

But they looked quite different from close quarters, and not friendly at all. Before moving to Dublin, Tess had spent most of her life in the countryside, but it had been broad, rolling farmland; small, closely-tended fields surrounded by straggly hedgerows. This was quite different. This was a wild and alien place. Small blackthorn bushes stood like squat sentries at every entrance, challenging her to brave their sharp weapons. Beyond them the interior of the wood was darkly green, full of shadows and silence.

Tess stepped back and made her way along the awkward stony ground at the woods' edge, hoping for an easier way to get in. Sometimes a stone wobbled or a stick cracked beneath her feet, and it seemed to her that she heard corresponding footsteps inside the woods. She stopped. The silence was complete. But as soon as she walked on she could hear them again, quite clearly this time; whispering footsteps on the soft woodland floor.

Again she stopped; again there was silence. Just ahead of her an entrance seemed to present itself; an opening like a dark tunnel, not obstructed by thorns. Tess hesitated. A blackbird gave an alarm call, a panicky rattle that seemed to tail off into a sinister laugh in the dark interior. Afterwards the flutter of bird wings sounded more like bats, and made Tess's skin crawl. She breathed deeply, trying to collect herself. It was only a wood, that was all. A quiet wood at the foot of a mountain. It couldn't possibly be dangerous.

But at that moment, as though to prove her wrong, something moved, gliding swiftly and silently among the shadows. Tess stepped back, unsure what she had seen. Whatever it was had walked on two legs, upright like a person. But it was vague and shadowy, too tall to be human and much too fast. What was more, it seemed to have antlers on its head.

Tess had seen enough. Her courage failed her and she began to walk quickly back the way she had come, glancing round frequently, her nerves on edge. Not until she was safely inside the boundaries of the farm meadows did she relax enough to stop and look back. From where she stood she could hear the anxious complaints of the gathered sheep and the irritated tones of Uncle Maurice's voice. The mountain was silvery-grey, its flowing lines graceful and soft, the woods at its feet grey-green and innocent. Tess wondered how she could have been so stupid. Surely there couldn't have been anything in those woods. It must have been her imagination. What was worse was that she had just wasted one of the last opportunities she was likely to have to make use of her Switching powers.

She would have gone back in the afternoon, or perhaps taken another route into the mountains, but her aunt, perpetually overstretched, collared her to look after Colm while she brought Orla to a local homeopath. Tess wanted to take Colm out for a walk or a game of football, but he was determined to stay in and watch his new *Star Wars* video, and when it was finished he wanted to watch *The Empire Strikes Back* as well. Tess watched with him, enjoying the films despite herself, and after lunch Uncle Maurice went out to meet someone on business and Brian joined them in the sitting-room. Colm didn't appear to understand a word of what was going on, but it didn't matter to him. He loved the little robot R2D2 and curled up with glee every time it uttered its electronic language of squeaks and bleeps. Tess laughed at his pleasure. There were worse things than having small cousins. Nonetheless she was uneasy. Time was running out.

That evening, Uncle Maurice was in an unusually cheerful mood. When he had finished his dinner he pushed his plate aside and said, 'Well, I've cracked it.'

'Cracked what?' said Aunt Deirdre.

'The sale of that piece of land. There's a developer in Ennis who is going to buy it off me to build a holiday village.'

Orla was always slow at eating, and this evening was no exception. Her plate was more than half full, but she put down her knife and fork in a very conclusive way. She looked across at Brian who, it seemed to Tess, had suddenly gone pale. He glanced back at his sister, and Tess thought she detected an expression of alarm in his eyes.

'You know. A place where tourists can come and buy a house, or rent one,' Uncle Maurice went on. 'Great spot for it. I'll be getting the deeds from the solicitor in the next couple of days. I'll need your signature, Deirdre.'

Aunt Deirdre nodded passively. But Orla said, 'Do we have to sell it, Daddy? Can't we keep it?'

'That piece of land is no use to us at all,' her father replied. 'You know that as well as I do. And think what we could do with the money!'

'But what about Uncle Declan?' said Orla. 'Couldn't we . . .?'

She got no further. If looks could kill she would have shrivelled in an instant beneath her father's furious stare.

'I'll not have that name mentioned at this table,' said Uncle Maurice, his voice conveying a growing danger. 'And as for the land, when one of you is running this farm let you run it as you want. In the meantime I'll make the decisions.'

His statement met with silence. Tess couldn't understand what was going on, but it was fairly clear that it was not a good time to ask. Her aunt was as white as the wall behind her. The rest of the family prayed that the fuse would go out before it lit the powder. And for once, it did.

After dinner, Tess went with Uncle Maurice and Brian to do the evening milking. Tess put out the nuts while Brian let the cows in. Bran and Sceolan made little rushes at their heels, but it was only for show. The cows knew exactly where to go and needed no encouragement. When the first lot were all in their stalls, Tess went round with the bucket of udder wash. Brian came along behind her, attaching the cups. Uncle Maurice stayed up near the machine's motor, checking that everything was going smoothly and doing a chemical test on the milk.

When the machine was set up and doing its work, Tess leant against the railings beside Brian.

'Why was Orla upset?' she asked. 'About your dad selling the land?'

Brian looked at her searchingly, as though he was trying to decide whether she was trustworthy. 'I suppose she thinks it's our land as well,' he said.

Tess nodded. 'Is it a big piece of land?'

Again Brian looked at her strangely, as though the information he was about to give was privileged in some way. He glanced around him, then shrugged.

'He has been wanting to sell it for years. Ever since he took over the farm from his father.' But if Brian planned to say more he didn't get round to it, because at that moment Uncle Maurice came marching towards them.

'Are you checking them?' he asked, knowing that they weren't.

Brian moved off and Tess followed, making sure that the cups were properly in place. The conversation had left her with more questions than answers, but her uncle seemed to be keeping a close eye on her and she couldn't get close enough to Brian to ask more. Some of the cows had finished their nuts, and turned to look at her as she worked around them. And although she had never found it very interesting to be a cow, she found their placid temperaments calming and she enjoyed their dry, philosophical humour. They had no language as such, but their expressions and movements told their stories. Best of all, Tess enjoyed the secret she learnt; that although Uncle Maurice considered himself to be their lord and master, they regarded him fondly as a rather bossy calf, who drank more milk than he ought to but was, like all young, ignorant things, tolerated.

When they had finished with the first lot of cows they moved quickly on to the second, and then the third. It wasn't long before the milking was over, and afterwards, while Brian and his father hosed down the floor of the shed, Tess went out into the yard.

The sun had dropped on to the horizon, where it sat like a vast, dazzling headlight. It lit the mountain in a way that Tess hadn't seen before, accentuating its faults and folds so that it looked pliable, more like flesh than rock. It made her feel strange, tingly, and the feeling intensified when she noticed a black bird approaching through the sky above the meadows. At first she took it for a crow, but as it grew closer she realised that it was far too big. It could only be a raven, and along with that realisation came another which sent shivers through her bones. She didn't know how, but she was quite certain that it was looking for her. As it flew over, it turned its head and looked down with one black eye, then wheeled above the farmyard, dropping lower, watching her all the time. The tingle turned to a bone-deep chill as the bird looked her straight in the eye, then swept up into the heights again, its huge wings making a whipping sound in the air. She watched it as it soared high and turned back towards the mountain, then she realised that she was not alone. Brian and Uncle Maurice had come out into the yard and were looking from her to the retreating bird with curious expressions. Then, as though in a conspiracy of silence, they turned and walked away from her, back towards the farm buildings. Tess wanted to call after them and ask them if they had seen what she had, but Orla emerged from the house.

'Want a game of Monopoly?' she said.

Tess stared at her, readjusting her mind to everyday existence. Her spirit was in turmoil, still disconcerted by the raven's visit but at the same time longing for the freedom to investigate. With an effort she managed a faint smile.

'Just one, then,' she said. 'If I can be the ship.'

# CHAPTER THREE

That night, it seemed to take forever to get dark. Now that there was no rain, the silence outside was profound; a mystery waiting to be explored. In the other bed, Orla wheezed painfully but, since she hadn't moved for more than an hour, Tess assumed she was asleep.

Something, a late bird or an early bat, fluttered past the window. Tess sighed and turned on to her back, willing the night to come. She wished that there was someone she could talk to. Not just anyone, but someone who would sympathise with what she was going through. Martin would understand; the boy who had learnt how to become a vampire but had opted in the end to be human. Lizzie would be all right as well, even if she did talk in riddles. But the person that Tess missed most of all was Kevin; her first and best friend. She wished she could see him now. She could imagine him sitting beside her, listening thoughtfully, understanding her frustration, knowing how it felt to be facing those last few days, knowing how difficult it was to come to a decision.

She realised that she was worried about him. Martin would settle down, sooner or later. He didn't admit it, but he was working hard at school, and he rarely needed to visit the counsellor who had eventually helped him to come to terms with the trauma of his father's death. His mother adored him and, although he was unlikely to be conventional, Martin would undoubtedly find a way to fit in and look after himself. But Kevin wasn't so lucky. When he had returned from his adventures and could no longer Switch, he had tried to rejoin his estranged family. It hadn't worked. They no longer understood each other, and Kevin couldn't fit in. Instead, he joined the increasing number of young people living on the streets.

He said it was different for him; said that he had spent much of his life scavenging as a rat and this was a kind of continuation of it. But from where Tess was standing it didn't look so noble. The streets and derelict buildings of Dublin provided a mean and cold existence for a boy, and although Tess helped him out as much as she could, she was afraid that if he didn't find a way of supporting himself he would sooner or later be compelled to turn to crime. And if that happened, Tess had no idea what would become of him.

Her thoughts were disturbed by a scuttling sound behind the wainscot. She sat up carefully, silently. There was an untidy hole in the boards where the radiator pipe had been brought through, relatively recently. As Tess watched, a brown nose and a set of twitching whiskers appeared, followed by a pair of bright, black eyes. Tess smiled, wondering how it was that her life had been populated by rats ever since she had first met Kevin. She was just about to address the newcomer in the visual language that she had learnt from the Dublin city rats when a door opened downstairs and Uncle Maurice's voice carried up the stairs, complaining about the film which had, apparently, just ended. The rat nose disappeared, but Tess's spirits lifted. Soon her aunt and uncle would be in bed, and she would be free.

When the human sounds finally came to an end, the rat sounds began. Tess heard the scuffles above her head as they left their nests in the roof-space and she listened to the rattle of loose plaster in the walls as they travelled down through the house. Before long, apart from Orla's breathing, all was quiet again. Still Tess waited until, eventually, she was sure that the household was asleep. Then she slipped out of bed and went to the window.

A gibbous moon was out, riding high above the mountains, making them seem closer than they were. A few small clouds hovered, becalmed, back-lit by the moon. Tess was torn between her desire to investigate the mysterious and beautiful woods and her fear of the gliding figure she had, or thought she had, seen. It would be better, perhaps, to return in daylight. In the meantime, a visit with the farmhouse rats would go a long way towards alleviating her boredom.

She was just on the point of turning back into the room when Orla spoke, sending an electric tide through Tess's blood.

'Tess?'

Tess caught her breath. 'Yes?'

'Can't you sleep?'

'No.'

'Nor me.'

Tess had a sudden vision of the two of them playing Monopoly until dawn. She prayed that Orla wouldn't think of it. But Orla had other things on her mind and Tess heard the familiar hiss and gasp as she took a dose from her inhaler. When she had let go of the medicated breath, Orla said, 'What are you looking at?'

Tess shrugged. 'I don't know. The moon. The mountains.'

Orla was silent for a moment and then, in a voice that betrayed a slight apprehension, she said, 'Do you believe in the Good People, Tess?'

'The Good People? Who are the Good People?'

'Fairies,' said Orla.

Another cold flush began in Tess's spine, but she caught herself and laughed it off. 'Fairies? You've got to be joking.'

But Orla didn't laugh. In the silence that followed her breathing became easier. Tess got back into bed and, seething inside, she waited. Her thoughts began to chase each other in irritated circles, but after a few minutes she was distracted by an unexpected sound.

At first she thought that someone had put on a video downstairs. The noise she was hearing was very like the musical bleeping of R2D2's electronic voice, and it was being answered by the polite, BBC tones of the other robot character, C3PO. But as she listened, Tess realised that the sounds were not coming from downstairs but from one of the other bedrooms.

She looked across the room. Orla was breathing freely and there could be no more doubt that she was asleep. Tess slipped out of bed again and crept out on to the landing. A dim light was always left on there, in case any of the children woke in the night. The sound of the *Star Wars* robots was still going on, and it was quite clearly coming from the bedroom which Brian and Colm shared, beside the bathroom. Furtively, Tess put her ear against the door and listened.

The boys must have been playing a tape. First there was a flurry of R2D2 bleeps and blips, then C3PO said, 'Oh, really, R2. We can't possibly do a thing like that!'

Another trill followed, like electronic birdsong, and C3PO replied again. 'Not tonight, R2. It would be far too dangerous!'

Tess was tempted to knock and join the boys, but she refrained. Better to stick to her own plan, now that she finally had the freedom to do it.

With the relief of a prisoner being released, she Switched. Even as she became a rat and began to adjust to her surroundings, processing sounds and smells, her human mind was wondering how she would survive when she couldn't Switch any longer. Like stepping back into prison, it would be. For a life sentence.

She put it out of her mind and concentrated on the present. Her rat body was supple and strong. She went silently back into Orla's room and slithered through the hole where the radiator pipe emerged. Then she was running and sliding down through the walls of the house. When she was human, Tess always thought that she could remember how it felt, but it wasn't until she became a rat again that she knew she was wrong. No memory could capture the immediacy of ratness or how it felt to be so small and yet so strong; so vulnerable and so brave. Why would anyone choose to be human, she wondered, if they could be a rat instead?

The first room that Tess came to was the sitting-room. She didn't go in. It didn't look like a promising place for foraging. There was only one rat in there as far as she could see. He was quite elderly and was having serious trouble with half a packet of fruit gums which were sticking his teeth together. He was scraping angrily at his jowls with his paws but was having no success. Tess noticed that he was missing one of his teeth; a top one, at the front. She wondered whether it was a casualty of an earlier fruit gum battle, but decided not to embarrass him by asking. She turned and slipped away before he saw her.

In the hall-way she encountered one of the strangest rats she had ever met. She was scurrying rapidly down the stairs carrying a bread-crust that Colm must have dropped on his rambles, and as she passed Tess she flashed an unusual greeting. Tess was pretty expert at the visual language that rats used to communicate with each other, but she had never been greeted like this before. The image was of a huge gathering of rats with Tess in the centre of it, being welcomed with joy on all sides. It was more than unusual. It was grand, larger than life, almost poetic. Tess watched as the other rat squeezed through a tiny hole at the bottom of the first stair, then she turned towards the kitchen. But part of her mind was still on the peculiar message, and she had blundered into the middle of trouble before she realised her mistake.

A mother rat had claimed the kitchen for her large, adolescent family and, for as long as they were in residence, it was a no-go area for other rats. Tess realised her mistake when the youngsters looked up from foraging around the bottom of the table legs and she found herself observed by nine practically identical faces. She turned to leave, but it was already too late.

There is nothing on earth more savage than a mother rat protecting her young. If they are threatened she will attack anything: a dog, a human, even a tractor. If she cannot stop the enemy, she will die in the attempt. In the scale of things, Tess was a pretty minor threat.

The mother rat hit her from above, leaping down from the sink where she had been keeping a careful look-out. Her weight, greatly supplemented by gravity, knocked the wind out of Tess and she was flattened for a minute, scrabbling uselessly at the slick lino floor with her claws. Above her, the mother rat crouched with bared teeth.

'Nanananana!' Tess sent rat images as clearly as her shaken mind could manage. She had a Rat name, that had been given to her a long time ago beneath the Dublin city streets, but now her mind hit upon a more appropriate nickname.

'Town Rat not hurting young rats,' she said. 'Town Rat not taking their food. Town Rat stupid; very stupid.'

She had managed to regain her feet by now, but kept her head on the floor and her throat bared in a gesture of absolute submission. Rats, Tess knew, obeyed nature's rules, one of which is that, among members of the same species, submission ends aggression. The only creatures that Tess had ever known to break that rule were human beings, but for a moment or two she wasn't sure that it would work. The mother rat took a menacing step forward and loomed over Tess. She must have been eating soap up there on the draining board; she stank of it.

'Nananana,' Tess pleaded. 'Town Rat going. Going very fast. Not looking back!'

The mother rat sent no images in return but continued to stare hard at Tess. Then, with no warning at all, she turned and walked away. Tess stayed where she was until the young rats converged on their mother in a clamour of admiration and anxious hunger. Then, with no pretence at dignity, she fled.

In the hall-way, at a safe distance, Tess stopped and groomed. With her teeth she chewed and combed her sleek, chestnut coat back into order. Then, after listening carefully for a while, she washed her face with the back of her paws. Finally, her self-respect intact again, she set off to have a look outside.

At the edge of the yard she searched long and hard with her eyes and ears, but there was no sign of the white cat. The last of the clouds had drifted away, and the sky was clearer than any she had ever seen. Despite the strength of the moon she could see stars; some close, some infinitely distant, like bright dust scattered across the night. Nearer, the mountains stood silvery and silent. They seemed to glow as though the eerie light originated with them and not with the moon. As she looked on, Tess was surprised to find that her rat mind was as capable of wonder as her human one. Where they differed was in their response to it. The human part of her was filled with impatient curiosity; a desire to explore and to understand. Her rat nature, by contrast, was content to experience the wonder, absorb it, and return to the important things in life.

Which, to a rat, usually meant food.

Tess's nose and ears soon told her where it was to be found. From the feed-shed at the end of the milking parlour she could hear delightful sounds:

hasty activity, gnawing and crunching and chewing, rodent jubilation. Hunger roared in her belly. To make herself look bigger and fiercer, she puffed up her coat, prepared to fight her corner if she had to. Then, twitching and bristling, she went to join the party.

# CHAPTER FOUR

But everything has a price. Breakfast the next morning was governed by Uncle Maurice's anger and, although Tess had been too tired to join him for the morning milking, she guessed what was on his mind even before he opened his mouth to speak.

'I've had enough of those flamin' rats. I'm getting rid of them once and for all. I don't care what it costs, I'm getting the exterminators in.'

Tess didn't know how pest control professionals went about their business, but she did know that they succeeded. If Uncle Maurice carried out his intention, most of the rats she had encountered the previous night would soon die a painful death. She shuddered at the thought, and Uncle Maurice caught sight of her.

'There's no point in being sentimental about it,' he said. 'It's all very well, you town folk coming in and thinking the countryside is full of cuddly creatures. Real life isn't like that, you know.'

Tess looked down at the table. She would never be able to tell him the reason why she was so horrified by his plans. Or what 'real life' meant to her.

'How come the cat doesn't keep them under control?' she asked.

'We have no cat,' said Uncle Maurice.

'But I saw . . .'

'I said we have no cat!'

Tess decided not to push it. After a moment, Aunt Deirdre breached the silence.

'I don't know about those exterminators,' she said. 'Are you sure the chemicals they use aren't dangerous? They might be bad for Orla's asthma.'

'Orla's asthma, Orla's asthma! I'm sick and tired of hearing about Orla's flamin' asthma. The rats have to go, right? If you can come up with a better suggestion, let me know.'

He stood up, pushing his chair back with such force that its feet grated on the flagged floor and made everybody's skin crawl. Then he was gone. Brian, who was his father's right-hand man, got up with an air of resignation and followed. One by one the other members of the family, even little Colm, let out a sigh of relief.

Orla was excused from washing-up because the detergent gave her eczema. She entertained Colm in the sitting-room while Tess and Aunt Deirdre cleared up. Tess waited for the effects of Uncle Maurice's outburst to clear and, when she felt her aunt had cheered up sufficiently, she plucked up courage.

'Who is Uncle Declan?'

Her aunt's mood collapsed again, as if she was a

balloon that had been punctured. 'Why do you ask that?' she said, and Tess thought she detected a touch of anxiety in her voice.

'No reason,' she said. 'Orla mentioned him, that's all.'

'I have no idea why she mentioned him,' said Aunt Deirdre. 'He isn't relevant at all. I have no idea what she was talking about.'

Tess waited, assuming that an explanation would follow, but it didn't. On the subject of Uncle Declan, Aunt Deirdre had said all that she intended to say. In silence she finished washing the dishes and in silence Tess dried them and put them away. Afterwards she slipped off again, quickly, before Orla could ask to come.

By the time she crossed the outermost boundaries of the farmland, Tess had already come up with a plan. Despite her fear she was desperately curious about the woods at the foot of the crag and she decided to use an alternative form to investigate. A bird of some sort would be ideal for getting a good look between the trees, and provided she didn't encounter that sinister raven, she should be safe enough.

A movement at the edge of her vision made her look up. A bright, red-brown hare was sitting on a rock a few yards away. Sensing Tess's eyes upon it, it froze, sitting upright on its haunches, still as the stones around it. Tess ached to Switch and join it, but she was still on the wide open hill-side. She could see no one, but there was no guarantee that no one could see her; from the height of the crag if not from the farmhouse. In the bright sunlight the fears of the previous day seemed absurd. Surely it would be safe enough to slip inside the edge of the trees, just long enough to Switch?

There was nowhere else. Her nerves on edge, Tess crossed the brittle rocks until she had reached the woods. Everything was quiet. She took a deep breath and, making herself as small and as nonchalant as possible, she manoeuvred her way past the sharp thorns and into the shadows beyond.

Straight away Tess knew that the woods were full of magic. The air was as fresh as spring water. There was a brightness about the leaf-filtered light that her eyes could barely contain, and a thousand vivid shades of green reflected it. Nothing was inert; the bark of the trees was like living skin, and the rocks were covered with velvety moss, like soft, green pelts. Between them the richly-scented earth was concealed by the leaves of wild strawberry and garlic.

Tess's fears evaporated and, overcome by the strange atmosphere, she moved forward. Here and there, in dry hollows produced by overhanging rocks or exposed roots, little heaps of empty hazelnut shells had been left by mice or squirrels. The entrances to more permanent homes had been dug out of earthen banks, and musky scents drifted on the air above them like signs, warning or welcoming. There was no evidence anywhere of human visitors; no discarded wrappers or tissues or cans; no paths; no fences; no carved initials on the trees. This was the wildest place that Tess had ever encountered.

Her heart filled with excitement as she wondered what shape to take on first. As if in answer to her question, the hare that she had seen earlier came into view again as it slipped silently away into the heart of the wood. Tess took a last breath of the cool, moss-scented air and Switched.

It was a long time since she had been a hare, and she had forgotten the lean, lithe strength of it, as different from a rabbit as a wolf was from a poodle. Her long hind legs were hard and tight, coiled springs waiting to unleash their power. She listened carefully for a moment and then, unable to resist, sprang into the air. She kicked and twisted, and barely touched the ground before leaping again, mad as a March hare. Once started she couldn't stop. Her claws tore holes in the moss and released the trapped scent of the soil, but soon this was overwhelmed by the rank smell of the garlic, bruised beneath the hare's strong feet.

'Tessss.'

She stopped, frozen to the spot, her big ears listening. Although her hare's brain could not interpret human speech, the sound of her own name was unmistakable to Tess. For a moment it seemed that the sound must have been her imagination, but then it came again, a sibilant, far-carrying whisper which seemed to originate all around her at once.

'Tessss.'

Someone was watching, someone who knew who she was and what she was doing. Her instinct was to Switch, and fast; a bird would be the best way to escape. But as though it knew her thoughts better than she did, the raven chose that moment to swish above her head, so close to the treetops that it almost touched them.

'Tessss.'

Her hare brain was urging her to run and she would have complied if her human brain could decide which direction to take. But suddenly, in her panic, she had no idea where she was, and which direction led to the crag and which led away from it. She found herself running, dodging between the trees, thwarting the hare's instincts and heading for light and open space. A moment later she was back at the edge of the woods, and as she burst out past the blackthorn she Switched. But the voice was still there, still behind her.

'Come in, Tessss. Come in.'

The thorns snagged at her clothes and her skin, but her momentum was too strong for her to be able to stop or even slow down and she landed hard on the stony ground beyond, winding herself badly. As she picked herself up and began to examine the thorn-wounds on her arms, the unmistakable sound of delighted laughter rang out through the woods.


Back in the farmhouse kitchen, the smell of fresh baking made Tess feel ravenous. Brian was pouring tea into mugs.

'What have you done to yourself?' asked Aunt Deirdre, pulling up Tess's blood-stained sleeves and examining her scratched arms.

'I'm OK, thanks,' said Tess. 'I just had an argument with a bush.'

Brian snickered and Tess made a face at him. She bit into a steaming scone and wondered why it was that food always tasted so much better after a spell in the open air. Through the window she could see Colm splashing about with a bucket of water and a plastic jug. The family weren't so bad, really, and for the first time since she had arrived Tess felt comfortable and relaxed.

'I went up into the woods,' she said. 'Over there at the bottom of the crag.'

Aunt Deirdre glanced at her sharply. 'You might be better to stay away from there,' she said.

Tess's skin crawled. 'Why?'

'She's scared of the fairies,' said Brian. 'Take no notice of her.'

A sudden flash of white at the window made Tess look up. The white cat was there again, sitting on the outer sill, staring in.

'There it is,' said Tess. 'I knew I'd seen a cat.' She turned to Brian, but he was giving her that look again, like the time in the milking parlour; a worried, mistrustful look.

'Pay no attention to it,' said Aunt Deirdre. 'It's only a stray. Would you like another scone?' But before Tess could reply, the domestic storm erupted again. Without warning, the door to the hall burst open and Uncle Maurice swept in, dampening the mood instantly and putting everyone on edge. Brian jumped up to get him a mug of tea.

'Four hundred quid,' said Uncle Maurice, bitterly. 'Four hundred, flamin' quid, just to get rid of a few flamin' rats!'

'My god,' said Aunt Deirdre, but it was more in the way of a practised response than a genuine expression of surprise.

'Four hundred quid,' Uncle Maurice said again. He seemed dazed.

'And what do they do for it?' asked Aunt Deirdre.

'They get rid of the flamin' rats, don't they?'

'I know that. But how?'

'How should I know? Poison them, gas them, I don't know.'

Tess felt sick. She would have to warn the rats in time.

'When are they coming?' she asked.

'Whenever I ask them to,' said her uncle. '*If* I ask them to. If I can find four hundred quid!'

'We'll have to find it,' said Aunt Deirdre. 'I'm sure they were in the house last night.'

'And there are two of them drowned in the water butt,' said Brian. 'There must be millions of them around the place.'

Uncle Maurice shook his head. 'We can't be living with that, sure,' he said. 'Four hundred quid or no four hundred quid, they'll have to go.'

When Tess had finished her tea, Aunt Deirdre asked her to hang out a load of washing on the line. She was just pegging out the last few things when Orla called her from inside the house.

Tess ran in.

'Your boyfriend,' said Orla, handing her the phone.

Tess scowled at her and shook her head. 'Hello?' she said.

'Is that Tess?'

'Kevin! That's amazing. I was just thinking about you.'

'I bet.'

'Well, it was yesterday, actually. But I was, honestly. Wishing you were here.'

'Well, then. Your prayers are answered. I'm on my way.'

'Oh, yeah,' said Tess, sarcastically. 'Sure you are.'

Kevin laughed. 'I am. I really am. I'm coming for a holiday. A guy I know has a van and he's coming that way. I've borrowed a bike and a tent off Martin. Do you think that I'd forget your birthday?'

Tess's heart warmed towards him. 'You're brilliant, you know that?' she said.

'Yeah. But unfortunately I'm not rich. I'll only have a few quid left by the time I've bought a bit of grub. Any jobs down that way?'

Tess knew that getting money out of Uncle Maurice was like trying to get blood out of a stone. But, for some reason, the figure of four hundred pounds popped into her mind.

'Not unless you can . . .' She stopped, thinking it through.

'Can what?' asked Kevin.

'Come to think of it,' said Tess, 'there just might be. If we play our cards right, that is.'

She looked up the stairs and at the closed door of the kitchen.

'Now, listen . . .' she said.

The day passed easily for Tess in the knowledge that Kevin was coming, and Uncle Maurice's moods didn't seem to dominate her own. She helped to treat the gathered sheep for foot-rot and dose them against worms, and afterwards volunteered to help mend a fallen wall.

Before long she began to wish that she hadn't. The stones were awkward and heavy, and Uncle Maurice seemed to assume she had prodigious strength.

'Flamin' goats,' he said. 'They're what has all the walls knocked on me.'

Tess said nothing, but heaved up another stone. Her one attempt at repairing the wall had resulted in a badly bruised toe, and she now left the building to Brian, who was surprisingly skilled at it. He took the stone from her and she stretched to ease her aching back.

'There they are, look,' Uncle Maurice went on. 'Up on the crag, see?'

Tess followed the direction of his pointing finger. Sure enough, she could just make out the multi-coloured forms of a herd of wild goats. The higher parts of the crag weren't quite as steep as the lower ones, but nonetheless the goats seemed to be standing at impossible angles as they browsed on the wild foliage.

Tess's heart went out to them and she longed to be there, climbing with them, breathing the rarefied air up there above it all. She cast her mind back to the morning's events and decided that she wasn't going to let fear cramp her style. They were among thousands of acres of farmland after all, and there were ways of getting up into the mountains without going anywhere near those creepy woods. A goat was one of her favourite creatures, and she wasn't going to miss out on the chance to be one again, perhaps for the last time.

But the opportunity took a while to arrive. After lunch they went to visit Uncle Maurice's parents, and then it was dinner time, and then there was evening mass. By the time Tess found herself alone again, night had fallen, and she was lying in bed, waiting once again for the household to sleep.

When, finally, all was quiet, she got up and, taking care not to wake Orla, crept over to the window. The moon was high and white. Beneath it the mountains gleamed like mercury, their strange, fluid forms giving the impression of melting. The beauty of the night took her breath away.

As she watched, mesmerised, she saw, out of the corner of her eye, a glimmer of bluish light somewhere around the base of the crag. She looked at the place where it had been, and immediately it flashed out in another place, just at the edge of her vision. A shiver ran down her spine. She blinked and rubbed her eyes to clear them, but again the spark-like lights flashed, first from one side, then from another. Like shooting stars, the flashes were gone before she could get a proper look at them, and they never seemed to appear where she happened to be looking at the time, but always at the edge of her vision.

She turned away from the window. She had intended to take on the form of an owl or some other nocturnal creature and make a night-time trip around the area, but now she wasn't so sure. There had to be an explanation for what she had just seen; a trick of her eyes, perhaps, or of the moonlight. But her rational mind was already way out of its depth and could make no sense of it at all. There was something in those woods that Tess couldn't begin to understand, and she had no intention of going out there in the dark, no matter what forms she had to choose from.

Much as she hated to admit it, Tess was afraid.

# CHAPTER FIVE

But in the morning, things, as they so often do, seemed quite different. Tess woke early, and the delight of the birds in the trees around the house made the fears of the night before seem like a childish dream. The morning was fresh and bright, and it was impossible for Tess to go back to sleep. Hardly daring to breathe, she slithered out of bed and began to gather her clothes. But it was already too late.

'Where are you going?' asked Orla.

Tess tried to hide her irritation. 'Do you never sleep?'

'Not much,' said Orla, truthfully. She coughed and sat up on the edge of her bed. Her legs, emerging from beneath her nightdress, were like pale twigs. Tess turned away. It must be awful to be so ill.

Orla began to pull on her jeans. 'Can I come with you?' she asked.

'Sorry,' said Tess. 'You know your mother doesn't allow you to come.'

'That's OK,' said Orla. 'She doesn't have to know, does she?'

Orla's face was lit with an illicit joy, and Tess felt panic closing in. Emotionally she felt compelled to take her cousin with her and look after her, but the last days as a Switcher were so precious to her that she couldn't bear to miss out on the chance to make use of them, not even for those few hours.

'Don't worry about my asthma,' Orla was saying. 'I'll bring my inhaler. I'll be fine.'

But Tess shook her head, hating herself as she did so.

'I'm sorry,' she said. 'You can't come.'

Orla stared at her in disbelief. In her chest something began to harden, and the first organ-squeak of a wheeze entered her breathing. 'Please let me,' she said and then, when Tess made no response, she went on, 'I'll take you to meet Uncle Declan.'

'Who is this Uncle Declan?' said Tess.

'You'll see,' said Orla. 'Just let me come. Please?'

Tess found that her curiosity about Uncle Declan had evaporated now that she knew he was someone who could be visited.

'Sorry,' she said again. 'Sorry.'

Bran and Sceolan whined from behind the closed door of their shed as Tess passed through the yard, but she didn't let them out. Her steps were heavy with guilt, but the morning was so inviting that they soon lightened. The dew was still lying in big, spangly drops on the grass, making the fields pastel-coloured and soaking Tess's trainers. She looked down at them as she walked, wondering what kind of feet she would be looking at after her birthday, the day after tomorrow. She imagined hooves there, horse-hooves, and remembered the feeling of head-tossing horseness; all pride and contained strength. She saw dogpaws, trotting tirelessly through endless miles, then cat-paws, graceful and silent. They were all so familiar and so precious. She realised as she walked that part of the difficulty in choosing what to be was having to give up all the other things. She didn't want her time as a Switcher to end. The realisation threatened to drown her in tears and she looked up, struggling hard against a growing sense of despair.

At least Kevin was coming later on in the day. The thought went some way towards cheering Tess up, and she set off again, turning to her right, away from the woods and towards another area of the stony wasteland beyond the farm boundaries. The new route took her over one of the walls that she had been mending the day before with Brian and Uncle Maurice. On the other side of it the sheep sprang up from their woolly huddle and stood glaring suspiciously, leaving behind a large patch of dry, warm grass. As Tess passed among them they waddled out of her way, shaking the sleep out of their fleeces and their small brains. The ewes, recently shorn, seemed puny beside their fat, woolly lambs. There was one certainty, at least; one animal that Tess would never choose to become. Maybe it would be easier to decide the end result by a process of elimination?

She wouldn't be a cow, that was certain, nor a pig. Not a gerbil either, or a caged bird, or any of those poor creatures that lived half lives in the service of human beings. Still deep in thought, Tess arrived at the further wall of the sheep meadow and climbed over it into the grey scrubland beyond. She was just coming to the decision that she would be a wild thing, in a wild place like this one, when a snort as loud and sudden as a pistol shot rang out through the still morning air.

Tess jumped, then froze to the spot until the source of the extraordinary sound became clear. Not far away from her was a small herd of wild goats. Some of them were standing on the rocks, others lying nearby, but getting up now and stamping and staring across the open space at the intruder. Tess kept still, aware that they were on the point of scattering and that one wrong move would set them off. Carefully she turned round and looked back. The house was a good distance away but she was not out of sight of it. The wall, however, was quite high and she could drop down and hide behind it if she was careful.

A moment later, the disturbing presence of the human girl was gone and a new goat emerged, as if from nowhere. The wild ones stared at it in astonishment for a few moments before overcoming their mistrust and moving hesitantly towards it. Tess waited, adjusting to the new situation and the altered senses, remembering how it felt to be a goat. The first to approach her was an elderly nanny. Her bones protruded, her coat was long and straggly and clearly she had seen better days. But her age had bestowed two things upon her. One was an enormous pair of horns and the other was an indisputable authority in the group. She approached Tess with an expression of lofty disdain, defying her to make a challenge. Tess did not take up the offer but made herself as unthreatening as possible, waiting for the older goat to make the running. She knew that each species in the animal kingdom had its own protocol, and she knew that in no case could introductions be hurried.

But on this occasion, the proceedings were brought to an abrupt end.

Tess heard the ominous rumble of stones at the same time as the other goats. Unfortunately, however, she had her back to the danger, and the entire herd had launched into a gallop like racehorses coming out of the starting gates before she had the faintest idea what was happening.

She followed. A goat's eyes, like most other herd animals', are on the sides of its head and not at the front, and Tess had often wondered why nature had not provided human beings with the same system. It had a few drawbacks in terms of close focusing, but it was brilliant for observation, since it provided nearly 360 degrees of vision. What this meant for Tess was that even as she ran she could see all around her without turning her head. And what she saw struck terror into her heart. For behind her, rapidly eating up the remaining ground, were a brown dog and a black one. Bran and Sceolan.

Uncle Maurice was up. He had set the dogs on them.

Tess ran as she had never run before. There was no time to think, or to plan any kind of a strategy. The chemical fear that surged through her body was like dynamic fuel. She had to expend it. She had to run.

The dogs were close behind her as she bolted across the scrubland. She was barely keeping ahead of them. Her hard little feet glanced off the bare rocks, wobbled loose ones and sent small ones flying. Her mind worked with lightning precision as she sped across the rough ground, leaping over bushes and avoiding the dangerous grikes which criss-crossed the

37

limestone like small chasms, incalculably deep. But the dogs were as fast, and as clever.

Ahead of her the other goats began to prove that they were not sheep and to separate off into pairs and small groups, all taking different routes, improving the odds. Tess, still at the back, followed on the heels of two youngsters of an age comparable with her own. They made a dart to the left, towards the woods and the crag and, without thinking, Tess stayed close, shadowing their progress. To her horror, the dogs stayed with them, too. She could hear their breath and sense their steady, sinister purpose. What was worse, she knew what it was to be a dog; how determinedly they could run, and how tirelessly.

Ahead of her the two young goats shot into the woods and disappeared. A moment later Tess was in there, as well, and close behind them. Then, quite suddenly, the other two jinked to the right and back towards the open. The movement was brilliantly designed to put the dogs off, but unfortunately it put Tess off, too. She couldn't follow fast enough and knew that she couldn't afford to hesitate, either. Alone now, the dogs still on her heels, she plunged on between the trees. And with a dreadful shock, she realised why the other two had turned back. They knew, and the dogs did, too, that this way was a dead end. It was only a matter of time before Tess's progress would be halted by the foot of the crag.

Her fear increased. She looked right and left but couldn't find the right opportunity to turn. Nor, with every nerve focused on flight, could she muster the presence of mind to Switch. They were going so fast that they were already approaching the cliff, and for a few awful moments it seemed to Tess that all her worries had been for nothing, since she wasn't going to make it as far as her birthday. As the grey rock-face began to show itself between the trees, the dogs moved out to flank her on either side, prepared for any swerve she might take in either direction.

There was only one choice left open to Tess. She would have to stand and fight. She had no idea what the odds would be, since she was young and her short horns had seen no action. But she was determined that the dogs wouldn't see the end of her without some fairly tough resistance. All at once the rock was rising sheer before her, and she was skidding to a halt in a flurry of moss and leaf mould when she heard an unexpected sound behind her; a savage snarl followed by an indignant yelp.

Tess spun round to see what was happening. To her amazement there were now three dogs instead of two. The newcomer was not a sheepdog like Bran and Sceolan but belonged to a far older breed. It was an Irish wolfhound; grey as the limestone, skinny and muscular as the goats. It was on the offensive; hackles raised, snapping and snarling at the astonished sheepdogs.

There was no competition. Bran was too old to put up a good fight and Sceolan was too young. As well as that, they were away from their own territory and on unfamiliar ground. They did their best to maintain their dignity, but backed down nonetheless and were soon trotting through the woods the way they had come.

The wolfhound watched them go, then turned back towards the place where Tess was standing. And, as it regarded her quietly with its brown eyes, she realised that she had made a terrible mistake. The hound had rescued her, or at least given her a reprieve, but it had not been done out of gallantry.

The look in those eyes was keen and hungry. This was not a well-fed farm dog out for a bit of sport but a lean, mean hunter, looking for a meal. Tess might be out of the frying pan, but she had jumped straight into the fire.

But she had, at least, that moment to act, and she did. The instant before the hound sprang she Switched into a blackbird and rose with a terrified chattering up through the branches and into the clear sky beyond. Once there she Switched again, and with sharp kestrel eyes she watched as the thin hound sloped off among the trees. As she hovered, still watching, her ears began to pick up a sound in the background that meant something. She was still shaken, and it was a moment or two before she could allow herself to let go of the fear of the chase and concentrate on the information. But the instant she did, a new shock went through her bloodstream. The sound was the hysterical yipping of a dog that had cornered its prey. Bran and Sceolan had found another victim.

# CHAPTER SIX

Still in the form of a kestrel, Tess climbed the skies until she could get a clear view of the surrounding wasteland. She did not have to rise very high in order to see where the noise of the dogs was coming from. For a moment she hovered, taking in the scene. The old nanny goat, the one who had first approached her near the farm wall, was facing Bran and Sceolan, who, despite having run down their quarry, weren't about to tangle with those well-practised horns. What Tess couldn't understand, though, was why the old goat had chosen that spot to make her stand. The ground there was wide open, and there was no way the dogs could have cornered her. It didn't make sense.

Then she saw. The goat's kid, one of the smallest of them all, had fallen into a deep grike and was trapped there, suspended between the sheer walls. And at the same time that she saw him, Tess's sharp hawk-eyes saw something else. Neither the goat nor her kid were in any immediate danger from the dogs, but Tess was not the only person to have heard the frantic barks. Uncle Maurice had heard them too, and was crossing the fields with a swift stride. Over his left arm, open at the breach, was his shotgun.

Tess began to act without stopping to think. Somehow, she had to get there before him. In the blink of an eye she had flown to the edge of the woods, then she folded her wings and stooped, dropping like a stone towards the rocky ground below. The fall was breathtaking, a kind of death-dive, and if Tess hadn't learnt to trust the instincts of her animal forms she would have been terrified. But the bird's senses were more accurate than any computerised landing system and, at the last possible moment, she opened her wings and broke the fall. Ducking sideways, she swept into the shadowy edge of the trees before landing and Switching, all in one motion.

Then she was running, as fast as she dared on the dangerous going. She was glad of her trainers. At home in Dublin she had a pair of fashion shoes with huge, chunky heels, but as she sped across the rocks she promised herself she would never, ever wear them again. You never knew when you might need to run; to save your own life or someone else's.

She glanced towards the farmhouse as she went. As far as she could make out, she was roughly the same distance from the goats as Uncle Maurice was, but she was travelling faster and would almost certainly get there first. He lifted a hand and waved at her, calling out something that she didn't hear but could guess. She looked away, pretending that she hadn't seen him, and raced on. Out of the corner of her eye she could see that he was increasing his pace, and before long he was across the boundary wall and moving rapidly over the rough ground.

Tess ran all the harder. Now she could no longer avoid hearing her Uncle's shouts.

'Tess! Stay away now, do you hear? Leave them alone!'

She was nearly there. Sceolan ran up to greet her, proud of himself, but Bran stayed where she was, holding the old goat, who stood with her horns down like drawn swords.

'Tess!' It was more of a scream than a shout, and now Uncle Maurice was running, scrambling over the flaking and wobbling rocks towards her and the stranded goats. But Tess was there first. Her heart was pounding, because she was running and because she was afraid. She was flouting Uncle Maurice, she knew, but there was nothing else she could do. If she obeyed him, stood by and watched while he shot the goat and her kid, she would never be able to live with herself.

Bran backed off and the old nanny ran a few steps when Tess arrived on the spot. She ignored them both and went for the trapped kid. As she knelt and grabbed it by the scruff of the neck it let out a harrowing bawl of terror, but a moment later it was free and speeding off across the rocks with its mother close at its heels. A few yards away, Uncle Maurice came to a halt. He raised the gun, but Bran and Sceolan were both in his line of fire, bounding after the goats.

Tess called them off and by the time they returned, willingly enough after their long ordeal, the goats were at a safe distance. Uncle Maurice lowered the gun and stared at Tess in impotent fury. Then he shook his head angrily, turned on his heel and marched off the way he had come. Apologetically, the dogs took leave of Tess and followed him.

She could understand why Uncle Maurice hated the goats. They knocked down his walls and stole the grass he needed for the sheep when grass was at its scarcest. She knew, as well, how she must appear to him; an interfering townee full of sentimental misconceptions about country life. She watched as he made his way home, the dogs at his heels.

They were going back to their everyday lives. So were the goat and her kid, who were already far away, two dots on the grey landscape. Everyone had a place in the scheme of things. They knew what they were and they accepted it and got on with it.

But not Tess. She was not of either world; the animal or the human. With a heavy heart, she sat down on a slab of limestone and waited for the trembling in her limbs to subside. Her birthday loomed, more like a funeral than a celebration, an end instead of a beginning. She didn't know who she was or who she wanted to be. When she tried to think of her life stretching ahead of her, nothing came. There was no picture, no purpose. Nothing fitted. Like a reflection of her dark thoughts, the raven flew over again.

Tess stayed out for as long as she could, delaying the time when she would have to go back to the farm and face the music. She would have liked to have spent more time as a goat, but the sour taste of the morning's experience stayed with her and she felt too downhearted to do anything adventurous. She spent an hour or two exploring the bottomless grikes from the thrilling perspective of a mouse, but eventually hunger drove her homewards.

It was nearly mid-day. She found Aunt Deirdre and Orla podding a bucket of peas.

'Can I help?' she asked.

Orla avoided her eye and said nothing.

'Have you had breakfast yet?' said Aunt Deirdre. She didn't sound very friendly, either, and Tess realised that her uncle had probably given them all a report of her rebellious behaviour.

'Not yet,' she answered.

'You'd better get yourself something,' said Aunt Deirdre, but she still didn't look up from what she was doing.

Feeling more like an outcast than ever, Tess made tea and toast to the rhythmical snap and rattle of the peas.

'Will you have a cup?' she asked the others.

'I don't mind,' said Aunt Deirdre, and at last Orla looked up and nodded and then, before she looked away again, she winked. Tess felt better, knowing that she had at least one ally in the house.

Soon afterwards, Uncle Maurice and the boys came back with a trailer-load of turf for the range. Tess went out to help with the unloading, but her uncle walked straight past her as though she wasn't there. Behind him, Brian shrugged and grimaced and, in the pick-up, Colm shrugged and grimaced in imitation.

Tess went back indoors. She had intended to explain about Kevin coming and to make much of his character and his abilities, but there was no point in trying to do that now. She was in Uncle Maurice's bad books and there seemed, for the moment at least, to be no way out of them.

So, instead, she got out of the way and lay on her bed and read a book. Before long, Orla joined her.

'I'm sorry about this morning,' said Tess. 'I know it was mean. The truth is, I just wanted to be on my own.'

Orla nodded, suggesting a forgiveness that Tess didn't feel she deserved. 'I saw what you did,' she said.

A chill ran down Tess's spine; the ever-present fear of discovery.

'What did you see?' she asked.

'With the goat and the kid,' said Orla. 'I was watching. Daddy gets so mad with the goats when they come anywhere near the good land. I was sure he was going to shoot them, and then I saw you come running out of the woods.'

Her eyes were glowing as she remembered the scene and Tess suddenly felt like a hero instead of a criminal.

'I was so afraid you wouldn't get there first. I was jumping up and down and shouting.'

Orla was gazing at the ceiling as she spoke, still full of the pleasure of victory. But abruptly her face changed as another memory supplanted the first. 'Daddy was very cross.'

She said no more, leaving Tess to imagine the scenes on his return to the house. For a long time they stayed quiet. Orla's breathing seemed to be worsening again, or maybe it was just that, because of the stillness, Tess was made more aware of it. From outside came the regular clatter of sods of turf being thrown into the fuel-shed. Then Orla spoke again.

'My grandmother told me that one time when her father was a young man his dog put up an enchanted hare.' She paused, perhaps to see whether or not she had Tess's attention.

'How did he know it was enchanted?' said Tess.

Orla sat up, all eagerness now to tell the story. 'He didn't at first,' she said. 'His dog caught hold of her by the heel but, good and all as the dog was, he wasn't able to keep a hold of her and she kicked free.'

Tess leant up on her elbow, aware of a strange thing that was happening to her cousin. Although her voice was as weak and breathless as ever, it seemed to have taken on a different intonation, even a different dialect. It was as though, in entering the story, Orla had moved backwards in time to another age, when stories were one of the only forms of entertainment. Lizzie's reference to ancestors flitted across the surface of Tess's consciousness, then was gone again. As Orla went on, the flow of words was smooth and seamless.

'She was wounded, though, the hare, and it was easy enough for the dog to turn her away from the woods, which is where she wanted to go. On she ran, and it seemed there was no cover in the world for her except for Josie Devitt's house.'

Orla stood up and moved to the window as she spoke. 'It's gone now, that house, but it used to stand over there.' She pointed and Tess joined her at the window. 'On that bit of grassy land there, where there's a clearing in the rock.'

Tess nodded, and Orla continued. 'Well. It happened that Josie was out and about on the land at the time, but the half-door of his house was open on account of the weather being fine for the time of the year. So up and over went the hare when she came to the house; up and over the half-door and disappeared inside. But the thing was, when my great-grandfather opened the door to let the dog in after her, there was no hare there at all, but only an old woman, and her leg all cut and bleeding.'

Orla stopped, and Tess thought she was pausing again. 'Go on,' she said. 'What happened?'

Orla shrugged. 'That's the story,' she said. 'That's all of it.'

Tess leant back, disappointed somehow.

'Do you believe it?' Orla asked.

Tess was tempted to explain that it was impossible; that she knew for a fact that no one could change their shape after the age of fifteen, but she refrained. Instead she said:

'I don't know. The old people were full of stories like that, weren't they?'

But Orla surprised her. 'I don't care,' she said. 'I believe it. It was a fairy hare and that's why I was glad you rescued the goat and her kid. They might have been fairy goats.'

'Well they weren't,' said Tess, feeling like a killjoy. 'They were just ordinary goats.'

'How do you know?' asked Orla, a hint of pique in her voice.

'Because there's no such thing as fairies, that's why. They're just old stories. From a time when people . . .'

'When people what?'

'When people were . . . less sophisticated, that's all.'

Orla was silent for a moment. Then she said, 'More stupid. That's what you mean, isn't it?'

'No. Not really,' said Tess.

But it was.

# CHAPTER SEVEN

Outside, the dogs huffed and then barked in earnest, their voices trailing off around the side of the house. Tess jumped up and looked out of the window, but all she could see on that side of the house was Uncle Maurice straightening up from the turf pile and heading around to see who was there. Colm, still cradling a sod of turf, followed on behind.

'Who is it?' Orla asked.

Tess shrugged and went out to the landing, Orla close behind her. The window there was above the front door, but it was already too late. Whoever had come was directly below, now, and too close to the house to be seen.

There was a knock at the door. Tess stood at the top of the stairs and listened as Aunt Deirdre answered it. She hoped that it wouldn't be Kevin. Not yet.

But it was. Tess knew it even before he spoke, by

the length of the silence while he waited for Aunt Deirdre to say that she had been expecting him. When, instead, she said, 'Well? What can I do for you?', Tess heard him stammer into life.

'Oh . . . Oh, well . . . em . . . I was wondering . . .'

'What were you wondering?'

Tess cringed. She knew she ought to try to rescue the situation and she was on the point of going down when Uncle Maurice came around the side of the house and took over the proceedings from his wife.

'What's going on?'

There was no way, now, that Tess could help. She closed her eyes and crossed her fingers.

But Kevin was thinking on his feet. 'I was wondering,' he said, 'whether you might be having a problem with rats? There's a lot of them about this year.'

'Are you from Pestokill?' said Uncle Maurice.

'No. I work for myself.'

'Oh yeah? And whose rats have you got rid of so far?'

'Oh, loads,' said Kevin, vaguely. 'Mostly in Dublin. I thought I might be more use down the country.'

There was a silence and Tess could imagine Uncle Maurice examining Kevin, weighing him up.

'Where's your gear, then?' he asked.

'On my bike.'

There was another long silence, and Tess felt she could almost hear her uncle's mind, calculating away. She knew what the next question would be before it came.

'How much?'

Kevin didn't hesitate. He had already discussed it with Tess over the phone. 'A hundred quid. Results guaranteed.'

There was another silence from Uncle Maurice, but it was shorter this time.

'How long will it take?'

'Not long,' said Kevin. 'I have a special technique. If you take me on, you'll have no rats here tonight.'

'And how will I know if they're gone?' he asked.

'How do you know you've got them?'

'Hmm,' said Uncle Maurice. 'Smart, aren't you? I'll tell you what. I'll give you a chance, all right? No money up front, though. I'm not thick. But if all the rats are gone from the house and buildings by this time tomorrow, you'll have your hundred quid. How does that sound?'

'Sounds fine,' said Kevin. 'I'll start now, if that's all right with you?'

'Fine by me. What do you need?'

'Just for you to put the dogs away. I'll do the rest.'

Tess turned back to the window and watched as Kevin scrunched across the gravel to where his bike was leaning against the wall. She noticed that the white cat had appeared again and was sitting on a low branch of the apple tree beside the feed-shed.

Kevin began to rummage in a small, dingy rucksack. At the corner of the house Colm, still clutching the sod of turf, stood staring at him, open-mouthed. Kevin winked at him and pulled out the thing he had been looking for. It was a small tin whistle.

Up at the window, Tess cringed. That was going too far. If this didn't work, Kevin was going to look like a complete idiot. For a moment she was glad that she hadn't acknowledged him. Below her, Uncle Maurice said to Aunt Deirdre, 'Pure nutcase.' Beside her, Orla was staring, wide-eyed.

'Who is he?' she said. 'What is he going to do?'

'I don't know,' said Tess. But the next moment,

Kevin demonstrated. He began to play the whistle, fairly tunelessly, and at the same time he began to call.

The part of Tess's mind that was and would always be rat tuned in instantly to the powerfully projected images; images that no ordinary human mind could receive. She was reminded that before Kevin reached the age of fifteen and lost the ability to Switch, he had spent more of his time being a rat than being a human being. His mastery of their visual language was total; far better than hers, and the messages he was sending were compelling.

'Out, out!' is what he was saying. 'Men coming with poisons, gases, traps. Rats dying in this place, rats dying in pain. Usguys leaving this place, huh? Huh? All of usguys leaving.'

Colm began to dance, clumsy in his wellingtons, curly locks flopping over his eyes. A moment later, though Tess had not noticed she was gone, Orla appeared beside him and began to dance as well. Infected by their enthusiasm, Kevin started to hop and skip, and Tess was sure that his playing became better; even tuneful. But she didn't listen to it for long. Beneath its cheerful tooting the more serious communication was continuing.

'Rats waking up, quick, quick! Rats coming out into the daylight, escaping deadly danger behind, yup, yup.'

Tess could hear her aunt and uncle snickering downstairs inside the front door, but a moment later they went deadly quiet.

Because it was working. Sleepily, shaking themselves awake, the rats were beginning to emerge. They crawled out of the subterranean world beneath the farm, and appeared by ones and by twos in the yard.

They scrambled and slithered their way down through the walls of the house, making so much noise that for an awful moment it seemed to Tess that the house was falling down around her. They surfaced from the drains in lengthening columns until suddenly the yard was flooding with rats, all blinking in the bright daylight and making their way towards the source of the urgent message.

Orla and Colm pointed and squealed in excitement, but they seemed unafraid and didn't stop dancing. Their views on rats, however, were clearly not shared by their parents. There was a blood-curdling shriek from the hall below as Aunt Deirdre realised what was happening, and a moment later, Uncle Maurice was striding across the yard, waving his arms around and making loud shooing noises. He swept Orla up under one arm and Colm under the other and carried them over to the oil tank, where Brian was already set up, enjoying a grandstand view of the action. Colm wriggled and kicked so hard that he lost one of his precious wellingtons, but once he was parked up on the tank beside his brother and sister, he soon forgot about it.

For now Kevin had begun to move off; still playing his strident and unmusical trills, still repeating his urgent warnings in Rat, but adding now a bit of more encouraging information.

'New homes, happy rats. Green woods, rats rolling in hazelnuts, fat and healthy.'

In the shed where they were locked, Bran and Sceolan howled and scratched and rattled the door. From his perch on the apple tree the white cat watched intently as the rats flowed along the ground behind Kevin like the train of a royal robe. Now that they were fully awake they were more organised, though still extremely perplexed. Kevin stopped for a moment to get his bearings, trying to remember Tess's description of the crag from their conversation on the telephone. As soon as he saw it he recognised it, and took the most direct route towards it; straight over the wall and into the first of the meadows. The rats surged over behind him like a single, slithering creature, and then they were gone, leaving the yard empty except for Colm's fallen boot.

The three children had jumped down from the tank and were heading off in pursuit when Uncle Maurice intercepted them at the wall.

'It's dangerous,' he said. 'Them rats could get nasty.'

So they clambered back up on to the tank and watched as the boy from nowhere receded towards the grey hills, dragging a strange brown carpet behind him. Not until he had disappeared beyond the furthest wall of the farm did they come down, and look around, and find to their amazement that life was exactly as it had been before he came.

Tess was in the kitchen garden, helping her aunt with some weeding when Kevin came back to collect his bike and his gear. He waved across and held out his arms in a questioning shrug.

She communicated with him in Rat so that no one else would know what she said. 'Morning, huh?'

'Morning, yup, yup,' Kevin returned. 'Tent in the trees, near the road, near the hump-backed bridge. Us two drinking tea together.'

Aunt Deirdre was looking at Tess in a quizzical manner.

'That boy's back,' said Tess.

'So I see,' said her aunt.

They both looked across at him again and, without her aunt seeing, Tess winked.

'Maybe it was something he had on him in the way of a smell or some such,' said Uncle Maurice over dinner that evening. Since Kevin's visit he had been in great humour, and if he remembered the incident with the wild goats, he did not mention it.

'I think it was that whistle,' said Aunt Deirdre. 'You know the way there are some notes only dogs can hear. Maybe it's the same with rats.'

'Could be, I suppose,' said Uncle Maurice. 'Where is he from, would you say? Do you think he's a traveller?'

Aunt Deirdre had no opinion and the conversation ended. Tess looked around at her cousins. Beside her, Colm was putting his dinner away with no fuss or mess, taking the business of eating extremely seriously, as usual. Opposite, Brian was engaged in his daily ritual of hide-the-vegetables; a wasted effort, since soon his mother would notice and begin the daily ritual of eat-the-vegetables. Beside him Orla, the special child, the sickly one, could get away with eating or not eating, whatever she chose. What she was doing with her food, however, was of no interest to Tess. Orla's face was lit up with an inner light; she wore an expression of almost saintly bliss. Tess looked away before her cousin could catch her eye. She understood Orla's feelings but they made her uncomfortable nonetheless. For Orla, without doubt, saw Kevin's removal of the rats as a demonstration of magic; further proof that there was truth in fairy tales. And Tess had no way of letting her know the plain and simple truth.

# CHAPTER EIGHT

That night, Tess took on rat form again and slid down through the walls of the house as she had done before. But unlike the previous night, the house was empty and silent. In the sitting-room a crumpled crisp packet smelt of heaven to her rat nose, but no one was there trying to get inside it. A few peanuts, dropped during the midnight movie, lay on the carpet beside the couch, untouched.

The kitchen was the same; empty and quiet. A new bar of soap sat beside the washing-up liquid on the draining board. Beneath the table half a dozen small cubes of cheese lay scattered on the floor, arousing a ferocious hunger in Tess's rat body and a strong sense of suspicion in her mind. There was something just a bit too neat about those blocks, as though they had been dropped there on purpose. What better test, after all, if her aunt and uncle wanted to find out whether or not there were any rats still around? So

Tess denied her hunger and backed off, slipping underneath the sink and down through the floor into the drains. A moment later she was outside and testing the night air with her nose and her ears and her whiskers.

There was no sign of the cat, and the dogs were safely locked away. Tess scuttled along the wall of the house, then crossed the moonlit yard to the buildings. In the feed-shed, the smell of the dairy nuts threatened to unhinge her. It was almost more than she could do to deny herself, and she might have Switched to avoid the temptation if she hadn't encountered something unexpected. In the corner of the shed, close to the feed-bins, a single rat was snuffling around short-sightedly. Tess recognised him immediately as the old, one-toothed lad she had seen in the sitting-room the night before, having trouble with the fruit gums. Clearly he had missed Kevin's call; maybe because he was old and image-blind, maybe because his sleep was just too deep.

When he caught sight of Tess, the old rat jumped, then ran forward delightedly to greet her.

'Every place empty, huh?' he said. 'House empty, yard empty, heaps of food and no one eating it.'

'Yup, yup,' said Tess. 'Rats gone, rats in new home in the woods.'

The old gentleman twitched his whiskers and sniffed the air.

'Rats gone, huh? Us two all alone, huh?'

Tess's heart lurched. She didn't know how to answer. For it wouldn't be the two of them staying behind but just him, abandoned and bewildered, completely alone for what remained of his life. It was too sad to think about, so instead Tess got busy, collecting the broken nuts that the broom had missed that morning and heaping them in a dark corner where her old friend could eat in peace. It was almost more than her rat mind could bear, to gather food and not permit herself to eat it, but it was vitally important that the old gent didn't go chewing at bags or leaving any other sign that he had been there. She had to pull out all the stops.

When at last she had gathered all she could, she left her friend chewing away in quiet contentment, and slipped out under the door into the yard. Back in the house she became human again and, still in the grip of rat hunger, did a thorough job of raiding the fridge.

Tess dreamt the dream again; the one in which Kevin was a rat. She woke in terror and sat up in bed. It was already light and the birds were singing their loudest and most delighted songs, which they only did on bright, clear days. Tess sat up and looked out of the window, trying to shake off the fear which still gripped her heart. Everything out there was normal and safe. And she had a plan of some sort; some reason to get up.

When she remembered, enthusiasm rushed in and washed away the sense of dread. She had arranged to meet Kevin. Wasting no time, she slipped out of bed and gathered her clothes. It seemed that Orla really was asleep. But as Tess looked down at her in the bed, she saw something that brought the fear straight back. On top of the covers and wedged against the wall was a book which, presumably, Orla had been reading the night before. The title was *The Old Gods: Story or History?* Beneath the title was a picture of a man, or something like a man, with antlers on his head. Tess turned away, but curiosity compelled her to turn back. The picture was just like the shadowy form that she had seen drifting through the woods the first time she had been there. She had assumed that she was imagining things, but if so, it was clear that she was not the only person who had imagined the same image. Why? Was it possible that such a being really did exist? With a shudder Tess tore her eyes away from it and crept out of the room.

She chose the kestrel again to find Kevin. The last time, she had been in a rush to see what Bran and Sceolan were up to, but now she could afford to explore the sensations of flight and the nature of the bird. Kevin had told her that another Switcher he had known had chosen a hawk as her permanent form when she reached fifteen. As she climbed into the heights Tess could easily understand why. The hawk was strong and clear-sighted. Tess always found the basic nature of animals and birds much simpler and less muddled than the complicated business of being human, but the hawk, above all others, had a purity of essence that was thrilling. The bird knew neither doubt nor hesitation; neither empathy nor remorse. Its eyes were designed for daylight but its heart belonged to the moon. Tess relished its sharp simplicity of being, and the knowledge that she might never experience it again made the sensations all the keener.

She could see the ground beneath her in the minutest detail. It wasn't at all like using binoculars; her sight didn't magnify the ground and make it seem nearer than it was. She just saw. She saw blades of grass, distant and tiny, bending beneath the weight of a stag beetle. She saw a bird tugging a worm from beneath a stone. She saw a matchbox toy, lost by some child many years ago and rusted now, barely visible among the grasses that had grown up over it.

Missing nothing, she climbed higher, widening her field of vision, scanning the landscape. She flew east and west, hovering occasionally to stabilise her vision, covering two or three square miles before the smell of smoke reached her and narrowed the search area. Eventually she found what she was looking for. Alerted by movement, she banked and overflew a stand of ash trees beside the narrow little bridge that Kevin had mentioned. Through the trees she could see the stretched dome of the tent and the resting spokes of the bicycle wheels. Delighted with herself, she dropped out of the sky, dodging through the branches at breakneck speed and coming to a hovering halt in the air, right in front of Kevin's nose.

Kevin jumped and took a step backwards, then realised who it was. He grinned and made a lunge at the bird, but she dodged out of his way and then Switched, judging the transition so perfectly that her feet met the ground as lightly as a feather.

'I keep forgetting you can do that,' said Kevin. 'Not fair.'

'Not for much longer, though,' said Tess.

Kevin nodded. 'Any plans?' he asked.

'No,' said Tess. 'It's driving me mad. What would you be if you had the decision ahead of you again?'

Kevin thought about it for a moment or two, then said, 'A rat. I always felt . . . I don't know . . . cheated, somehow. Because of being forced into a decision when it was time for me to choose. I'm sure that if I'd had a chance to think I would have decided on a rat.'

His words gave Tess an uncomfortable reminder

of her dream, but she said nothing and Kevin went
on, 'Maybe it doesn't make that much difference, in
the end. I mean, the best thing was being able to
Switch. Nothing could be as good as that, really,
could it?'

Tess sighed. 'It's like having everything, isn't it?'
she said. 'I can't stand the idea of losing it.'

Kevin had a neat little campfire going in front of
his tent, carefully confined inside a ring of stones.
On top of it a billy of water was coming to the boil.

'Tea?' he asked.

Tess sat down on a stone. As though it saw her, the
smoke changed direction and drifted into her face.
She waved her hands at it and waited. Sure enough,
it soon returned to its previous course.

'Anyway,' said Kevin, dropping a fistful of tea
leaves into the billy, 'what happened? How come you
didn't warn them that I was coming?'

Tess groaned and related the story of Uncle
Maurice and the wild goats. As she told it Kevin
nodded, understanding and approving in a way that
no one else ever did or could. Their friendship
warmed her heart as it so often had in the past. As
time went on it became more valuable, not less, no
matter how different their lives appeared to be.

In the silence that followed the end of Tess's
account, Kevin rooted around in his rucksack and
found another cup. Tess watched him. He was still
as tough and as scruffy as the town rats which had
been his main companions during his Switcher days.
He would never fit into normal human society, not
in a million years. In a sudden, uninvited leap of
imagination, Tess saw him as an old tramp, a bag
man rummaging around on the edges of society; a
human rat, unloved and unwanted. She had seen

people like that, adrift on the city streets. They existed without the anchors that kept most people stable: family or education or job. Tess wondered whether their minds drifted in the same way, untethered, unfocussed, unaware of time.

'Maybe it's best to leave it that way,' said Kevin.

Tess came back to reality with a jolt. 'What?'

'No need to tell them now that you know me, is there?'

'No,' said Tess. 'In fact it would be a bit awkward, since I didn't say anything yesterday.'

Kevin used a grimy T-shirt to protect his fingers from the heat of the billy as he poured the tea into two battered enamel mugs.

'Trouble is, though,' Tess went on, 'I won't be able to invite you to my birthday party.'

'Are you having one?'

Tess shrugged. Kevin spooned milk powder into the cups. 'We can have one,' he said. 'Just you and me. A midnight one.'

'That would be good,' said Tess. 'That would make everything easier.'

'It's a date, then,' said Kevin, then blushed. 'I don't mean that kind of a date. I mean . . .'

Tess laughed, but she could feel herself colouring as well. For a moment each of them struggled separately, trying to think of something normal to say. Tess got there first.

'What do the rats think of the woods?' she asked.

Kevin burst out laughing. 'They were very funny,' he said. 'They were like a coach-load of middle-aged tourists who have been brought to the wrong hotel.' He lapsed into fluent Rat as he continued. 'Feed-shed, huh, huh? Soap? Cupboards?'

Tess laughed.

'Usguys wet and cold,' Kevin went on. 'Usguys breaking our teeth on hazelnuts!'

If anyone had been watching through the trees they would have thought the two friends were quite mad, sitting in silence and laughing at nothing at all. But they understood each other perfectly.

'Blackberries sour! Yeuch! Hard work hunting, hard work making new nests!'

Tess could visualise them; fat pampered house rats, amazed at the lives their forerunners led, returning with the utmost reluctance to their wild roots.

'Will they stay, do you think?' she asked, returning to human speech.

Kevin nodded confidently. 'For a few generations at least. I painted a ferocious picture of Pestokill. They'll be telling their children and grandchildren about it. Like the bogeyman.'

Tess finished her tea but declined the breakfast that Kevin offered, not because the bread was squashed and the butter was full of grit but because she felt it would be better politics to make an appearance at the house.

'See you later,' she said.

Kevin was trying to cut the bread with a blunt knife, but he looked up when, a minute later, Tess was still standing there, as if undecided.

'You OK?' he asked.

Tess nodded. 'I was just wondering,' she said.

'Wondering what?'

'Did you see anything in the woods? Anything strange?'

'Not exactly. But there was a funny feeling about the place. I didn't really want to go in. Just left the rats at the edge like you suggested. Why?'

Tess shook her head. 'Just wondered.'

'Did you?' Kevin asked.

'I'm not sure,' she said. 'It was probably just my imagination. Maybe we could go there together some time?'

'All right by me,' said Kevin.

'It's a date, then,' said Tess.

Then, before Kevin could question her more closely, she Switched into a hawk again and sprang away into the sky.

# CHAPTER NINE

Uncle Maurice was in much better humour that morning. He was so cheerful, in fact, that Tess was suspicious. Something had to be wrong.

She helped him, all the same, as he finished the milking.

'You're up early,' he said. 'Do you always get up so early? At home, I mean?'

'Not usually,' said Tess, pulling open the sliding door of the milking parlour to let the last of the cows go out. 'Specially not at weekends. It's different here, somehow.'

'It is,' said Uncle Maurice. 'The light is different. It comes earlier in the country than it does in the town.'

It didn't, but Tess knew what he meant. There was a clarity about the dawn and an urgency in it. Maybe it was the racket that the birds made, or the fact that no buildings or exhaust fumes obscured the sun.

Maybe it was none of those things, but Tess's own urgency; her knowledge that time was running out.

Her uncle's voice disturbed her thoughts. 'What do you make of that boy, then?'

'Which boy?'

'The lad that took the rats away. Did you see that?'

'I did. It was amazing, wasn't it?'

'Amazing is right,' said Uncle Maurice. 'Would you say he could do it again? In another place, like?'

'I don't see why not,' said Tess.

'No. I don't either.' He took the pipe out of the creamery tank and connected the milking system up to the tap to be cleaned out. He was whistling as he worked, uncharacteristically happy. There was definitely something wrong.

After breakfast, Tess and Brian shared the washing-up. Orla sat in the corner of the kitchen wheezing, and reading the book with the deer-man on the cover.

'Did you ever read this, Tess?' she asked.

Tess shook her head. 'We did a lot of that stuff in primary school,' she said. 'I've forgotten most of it now.'

'You should read it,' said Orla. 'It's all about the *Tuatha de Danaan*.'

The mention of the name of the old gods of Ireland sent one of those electric feelings up Tess's spine, but before she could analyse it she was distracted by an excited yell from Colm outside. Brian ran to the front door and, when he didn't come back, Tess and Orla followed.

The source of Colm's excitement was Kevin, who was just arriving at the yard gate on his bicycle. Colm was there before him and had climbed up to the top bar when Uncle Maurice caught up and gathered him into his arms. It seemed that everyone was converging on Kevin.

'Come in, come in,' said Uncle Maurice, setting Colm down and opening the gate. Again his cheerful mood set alarm bells ringing in Tess's mind.

'Come in till we get a cup of tea,' he went on, leading the way into the house. Everyone followed except for the ever dutiful Brian, who was left with the job of closing the heavy gate.

Aunt Deirdre had come in from the garden and the kettle was already on. Kevin sat down at the table or, more accurately, he slumped. Tess was so accustomed to seeing him that she hadn't noticed the changes in his body, but all of a sudden they had become obvious. He was like a bag of bones, big bones, all loosely connected and not very well coordinated. His feet were enormous and his hands were long, with knuckles everywhere. He seemed acutely embarrassed by this strange body but it would, Tess realised, soon begin to make more sense. The hollows would flesh out and the shambling slackness would turn to smooth strength. Kevin was growing out of being a boy and would soon be a man.

The dawning truth was a shock to Tess. Kevin shifted uncomfortably and she realised that, while the rest of the family had been bustling about getting comfortable, she had been staring at him. She turned away quickly and helped her aunt to get out cups and biscuits. Uncle Maurice was settling himself into a chair opposite Kevin. As Tess poured milk into a jug and set it down on the table he began to speak.

'Have you done much of it, then? This rat clearance?'

Kevin tapped his fingers on the table and watched them. 'Not so much, really,' he said.

'You wouldn't be well known, then? Around the place?'

'No. I wouldn't be, I suppose.'

Tess set out the cups. She didn't like the way the conversation was going. Uncle Maurice nodded, absorbing what Kevin had said. In the brief silence, Colm climbed on to a chair beside Kevin and reached across the table for the best biscuit; the pink wafer.

'Colm!' said his mother, in a warning tone.

But if Colm heard her, he made no response. He continued with what he was doing and, to everyone's surprise, handed the special biscuit to Kevin. His face was as pink as the biscuit, glowing with shy charm. When Kevin shook his head his face clouded over with disappointment.

'He wants you to have it,' said Brian. 'He'll be disappointed if you don't.'

Kevin took the biscuit and ate it. Uncle Maurice began again.

'Where do you live, then?'

'Dublin,' said Kevin.

'On holiday down here, are you?'

'Sort of,' said Kevin. Tess made a point of not looking at him, but from the corner of her eye she could see that he was acutely embarrassed by the continued attention of the children. Colm was standing on the chair and gazing into his face with undisguised adoration. At a slightly more respectful distance, Orla and Brian were also staring with admiring expressions. It was clear that, as far as the younger members of the family were concerned, they were entertaining royalty. But Uncle Maurice was not of the same opinion.

'Are your mother and father on holiday with you?' he asked.

It was one question too many. Kevin stood up. 'If you don't mind,' he said, 'I'll take my money and get on my way.'

'Ah, now,' said Uncle Maurice, standing up as well. 'No need to be hasty. I didn't mean to pry. Sure, what does it matter, anyway?'

Aunt Deirdre spoke for the first time. 'Have your tea, now. 'Tis made and all.'

She poured it out and Kevin sat down again, reluctantly. Colm handed him another biscuit, a jam one. The silence while he ate it threatened to be a long one, and Tess broke it before it became too awkward.

'You have great weather, anyway. For your holiday.'

'I have,' said Kevin.

'He has, he has,' said Uncle Maurice and Aunt Deirdre together.

The silence fell again and Uncle Maurice finally got round to saying what was on his mind. 'No,' he began. 'It's only . . . Just . . . I thought you could make a great business out of that rat-catching game.'

'I could, I suppose,' said Kevin.

'If you had the right backing, that is. The right kind of manager.'

Tess turned away to hide the expression of disgust on her face. So that was what he was up to.

'I'm not sure,' Kevin began, but Uncle Maurice had launched his campaign and could no longer stem his excitement.

'No, c'mere, listen,' he said. 'I could get the world of business for you, the world of it. There are loads of farmers and houses in towns and all, and they have the same problem. Sure, a cure for rats is worth a fortune. A fortune!'

Tess looked around the room. Kevin was dumbstruck and she could only imagine what was going through his mind. From the expression on Aunt Deirdre's face it was clear that she hadn't been let in on the plan and was as surprised as everyone else. Once more Kevin opened his mouth to say something, but Uncle Maurice was still not finished.

'Think of it, lad,' he said. 'If you can do a farm and buildings this size, what's to stop you doing a whole village or even a small town? Can you imagine it? We could get TV people there and radio. We could set up interviews and all . . .'

Kevin stood up, his tea untouched.

'Thanks for your concern,' he said. 'It's a great idea but I'm afraid I have no interest in it.'

Uncle Maurice shut his mouth and the brightness left his features with frightening speed. Anxiety, almost visible, crept over the other members of his family.

'So if you'll just pay me what we agreed,' Kevin went on, 'I won't take up any more of your time.'

There was a sinister pause, then Uncle Maurice said, 'What was it we agreed, exactly?'

'One hundred pounds,' said Kevin.

'One hundred pounds,' Uncle Maurice repeated. 'If you got rid of all the rats.'

'That's right,' said Kevin.

There was menace in Uncle Maurice's voice as he replied. 'But you didn't, did you?'

Silence dropped again. The faces of the children showed shocked disappointment, but Kevin was not going to be fobbed off without a fight. 'What makes you say that?' he asked.

'Just this,' said Uncle Maurice. He stood up and went over to a plastic bag which lay inside the back door. 'Something the dogs caught this morning.' He reached into the bag and pulled out the carcass of a rat. A jolt of pain caught Tess off guard.

'That . . .' she began, but stopped herself while she still could. What she had started to say was that she recognised the carcass. It was the old rat, the one who had been left behind.

The others were still looking at her expectantly, even Kevin.

'That's what?' said Uncle Maurice.

In the nick of time it came to her. 'That's been dead for a couple of days,' she said. 'I saw it round behind the milking parlour yesterday.'

Kevin shut his eyes in relief and took a deep breath.

'Oh, is that right?' said Uncle Maurice. 'Well, you'd know, I suppose.'

Tess said nothing and the only sound was the high-pitched drone of Orla's constricted breath. Uncle Maurice followed up his advantage.

'I mean,' he said, 'you'd know the difference, wouldn't you, Miss Cleverclogs, between this dead rat and any other dead rat.'

He looked around triumphantly, as though expecting applause. But he hadn't won, yet.

'I think I would,' said Tess. 'I think that rat has only one top tooth at the front.'

Uncle Maurice's mouth dropped open in astonishment. But Brian was already at his side and staring into the slack mouth of the dead rat. Rapidly, Uncle Maurice dropped it back into the plastic bag, but he wasn't quick enough.

'Yep,' said Brian. 'She's right. Only one front tooth. How did you know that, Tess?'

Colm had understood little of the preceding conversation, but no nuance of mood or atmosphere ever escaped him. He knew now that his hero had been vindicated and he was delighted. An affectionate soul at the best of times, he flung his arms around Kevin's neck and hugged him tight.

But it was not a wise move, given the circumstances, and not only because of the embarrassment it caused Kevin. Uncle Maurice was a tyrant, without doubt, but he loved his children with a fierce passion. To see Colm's affection so freely given to his adversary was more than he could stand.

'Get out,' he said, his voice low, his face dangerously dark.

Kevin gently disengaged himself from Colm's embrace. As she watched, Tess saw the best of Kevin's rat nature emerge; his courage and, above all, his sense of justice.

'I'll leave when I've been paid,' he said.

'You'll leave right now,' said Uncle Maurice. 'Right this minute. And if I see you around here again I'll call the police.'

'The police? On what charge?'

'Loitering. Harassment. Whatever I like. Do you think they'll believe you for one minute? That you played on a tin whistle and the rats followed you out of my yard? They'll lock you up, more like it.'

Kevin stared at him in silent anger and Tess saw that he was defeated. Everyone knew that he was right, but that against Uncle Maurice's word he hadn't a leg to stand on. For a long moment, time seemed frozen in the room. Then Kevin strode to the door and was gone.

'Good riddance,' said Uncle Maurice, throwing the dead rat in its plastic bag out after him. But everyone knew that the matter was not closed, and the silence which still hung in the room was full of gloom and foreboding.

# CHAPTER TEN

If Tess thought that the bottom had fallen out of her world, she was wrong. The worst was still to come. The dust had barely settled behind Kevin's bicycle on the drive when a Mercedes car pulled up and two men in expensive suits got out.

Uncle Maurice threw the door open wide and went out to meet them, then preceded them into the kitchen where Aunt Deirdre, yet again, put on the kettle.

'Deirdre, this is Mr Keating from Keating Development.'

'Pleased to meet you,' said Mr Keating. 'But don't make any tea for us.' He gestured to the other man and turned back to Uncle Maurice as he spoke.

'This is Peter Mahon, the surveyor I was telling you about. We've come to walk the boundaries of that land, if it suits you.'

Tess had no interest in what was happening and

was about to slip out when the reaction of her cousins changed her mind.

'Can we come, Daddy?' said Orla.

'Please?' said Brian.

'Sure, we're only walking around the land,' said Uncle Maurice.

'But we love the crag,' said Orla. 'We won't get in your way. Honestly.'

'The crag?' said Tess.

But no one heard her. Uncle Maurice had given his permission, and the children were cheering and racing off to get their boots. Tess followed them into the hall.

'Did you say the crag?' she asked.

Orla nodded.

'You mean the land up there?' Tess pointed in the direction of the mountain, though all that could be seen was the wall of the kitchen.

'Yes,' said Brian. 'We're going to play around up there while they walk the boundaries.'

'But,' said Tess. 'Wait a minute. You mean that's the land that your dad was talking about?'

Orla nodded, a little sadly. 'Want to come?' she asked.

Tess didn't answer the question. She was still finding it difficult to believe what she was hearing. 'You're telling me your dad owns that wild land up there under the mountain. And he's selling it?'

Brian nodded. 'There's no point in trying to make him change his mind,' he said. 'He hates the place. He's been trying to sell it since he inherited the farm. He says he'll take us all on holiday with the money.'

Tess thought back to her experiences of the place. Despite her fear of it, the thought of those wild and beautiful woods being bulldozed and turned into a holiday village filled her with horror.

'But all the wild creatures who live there . . .' she began, then stopped, remembering the rats and the promises that Kevin had made to them about their new home. Her cousins were staring at her, waiting for her to finish. When she said no more, Brian said, 'Come with us, Tess. Please.'

Tess climbed into the back of the pick-up with the others, and they set out along the much longer road route to the crag. Behind them the developer and the surveyor followed in their smart, black car. From the mood of her cousins, Tess couldn't be sure whether it was a tragic occasion or a joyful one. It seemed to be both; their excitement at going to the crag counterbalancing their sorrow at having to part with it. Orla was still wheezing slightly but her cheeks, for a change, had a bit of colour. Little Colm spent the whole journey jumping around. Occasionally his red wellies missed their aim on the metal floor and landed on someone's toe, but no amount of complaining could persuade him to sit down.

Tess craned her neck and looked out through the front windscreen, hoping to catch a glimpse of Kevin, but there was no sign of him. She tried to imagine how he must be feeling; how full of anger and bitterness, and she wished that she had decided to go and look for him instead of coming on this family outing. Apart from the irritation of her cousins' manic mood, she was wasting precious Switching time. Like a dark cloak her worries began to close in again and she concentrated on the road ahead.

They were just turning down the stony track that led from the back road to the land around the crag.

Behind them the developer followed a bit more slowly, mindful of his suspension. On either side of the track tall hedges of hazel grew up, obscuring the view of the surrounding wilderness and creating a closed-in, tunnel-like effect. The bumpy ride meant that Colm's balance went haywire, but he still couldn't be persuaded to sit still and he ended up pitching wildly from one lap to the next. By the time they finally came to a halt, Tess was suffering from a combination of cabin fever, claustrophobia and bruising. She couldn't wait to get out.

But after the noisy ride, the atmosphere of the crag was uncannily silent. It was a silence that seemed to demand respect, and there was no one in the party who was not sensitive enough to become quiet in response. It was almost as though someone or something was present in their midst, and it made Tess uncomfortable. She looked around at the other members of the party. Her cousins looked thrilled, their eyes bright with excitement. The businessmen looked bewildered, as though they had expected something entirely different. But it was Uncle Maurice's reaction that made a shiver run down Tess's spine. He was standing beside the pick-up, still holding on to the handle of the door as though he wanted to be ready to get back into it in a hurry. The apprehension on his face was almost painful until he noticed Tess looking at him and, with a visible effort, he disguised it.

What was he doing? Did he know about the strange things in the woods as well? If he did, how could he allow his children to come there, and how could he sell the place?

'Right so,' he said, briskly. 'Where do you want to start?'

While the surveyor sorted out his maps and got his bearings, Orla led her brothers off across the rocks.

'Not too far, now, you hear?' said their father.

'OK,' said Orla. 'Come on, Tess.'

Reluctantly, Tess followed.

The place where the track ended and the cars were parked was to the far left of the crag. The mountain rose away less steeply there and the woods were just beginning like the point of a triangle. Orla led the way across the rocks, keeping the crag and the deepening woods to her left. Tess was relieved about that. Although her cousins clearly knew the place better than she did, she couldn't help feeling responsible for them since she was the eldest.

They hadn't gone far when Tess spotted the raven. It was circling above the adults, as though it was checking out what they were doing there, and as she watched, it changed tack and drifted above her, turning its head to look down with its sharp black eye. She looked away only to find, to her amazement, that all three of her cousins were waving cheerfully at the menacing bird.

'What are you doing?' she asked. 'Are you mad?'

But Brian winked, and Orla put her finger to her lips and said, 'Shh.'

To their right, Uncle Maurice and the businessmen were following the boundary wall, which led them away from the children at a wide angle. Still Orla continued along the bare rocks beside the woods. By the time she came to a stop, her father and his companions were three hundred yards away across open country.

Orla changed direction and walked towards the woods. Tess and the others followed. At the ragged tree-line they stopped and looked into the green shadows. Tess felt the familiar ambivalence; the magical attraction overshadowed by fear. Bird wings fluttered loudly among the branches. Orla turned to her and smiled delightedly. If she felt even the slightest anxiety she did not show it, and nor did her brothers. Once again, Tess found herself wondering if her experiences of the place owed more to an over-active imagination than to reality.

Colm led the way in among the trees and Orla and Brian followed. Tess was about to take her first step when she saw, or thought she saw, a vague figure standing in the shadows.

'Wait!' she hissed. The others stopped. She could just make out, far away within the dappled green interior, a figure just that bit too tall to be human. His face was turned towards the newcomers, but he seemed to be made not of flesh but of shadow and light. Tess strained her eyes, trying to get a better view. Was it a trick of the leaf-filtered sunlight, or was there a pair of antlers growing from the figure's head? As she watched he lifted a translucent hand and beckoned.

A cry pressed at Tess's throat but she held it back.

'There! Do you see?' she said to the others. But to her horror they were already moving, running with surprising agility over the mossy rocks and among the trees, straight towards the terrifying figure.

'Stop!' she shouted. 'Wait! Don't you see him?'

Briefly, Orla halted and turned back. 'Of course we do!' she called. 'Come on!'

Above their heads a brilliant light suddenly shone out from the level of the deer-man's eyes, blinding Tess so that she lost her bearings and had to hold on to a tree. The sensation was so disorientating that she wondered whether it was really happening or whether she was suffering from some sort of seizure; a migraine perhaps, or an epileptic fit. By the time her vision cleared, all she could see were branches and occasional flashes of bright, dazzling sunlight between them. There was no figure among the trees. There were no children, either. The woods appeared to be empty.

'Orla?' she called. 'Orla? Brian?'

There was no answer. Abruptly Tess's nerve failed. She turned and, despite the rough going, ran. Uncle Maurice saw her coming and met her halfway across the intervening space. Panting hard, he grabbed her arm so tight that it hurt.

'What is it? What happened?' he said.

'They're gone. They disappeared,' said Tess.

'What do you mean, disappeared?' said her uncle. 'Where?'

'Under the trees,' said Tess. 'I got dazzled. I . . .'

She stopped, aware that her uncle's attention had shifted. He was looking towards the woods, and Tess followed the direction of his gaze. To her amazement and relief, Kevin was standing on the limestone slabs at the edge of the trees. It made sense of everything. The strange figure in the shadows must have been him all along, and the antlers just a trick of the light.

Tess was about to call out to him when she remembered that she wasn't supposed to know him. Then she noticed that there was something odd about the way he was behaving. He was waving over at them, a strange little grin on his face, as though he was sneering. As they watched, the businessmen caught up with them, so there were four witnesses to what happened next. In a gesture whose meaning was unmistakable, Kevin snubbed his nose at them and vanished among the trees.

# CHAPTER ELEVEN

They searched for hours. Tess stayed close to Uncle Maurice, whom she felt safe with despite his foul temper. The businessmen made up a second party to scour the woods. Backwards and forwards they went, lengthwise and crosswise and every possible way in between, until the place became as familiar to Tess as her own back garden. But there was nothing to be seen or heard. No children, no wolfhounds, nothing. Even the wild creatures and the birds stayed silent, so that it seemed that there could be nowhere on earth more tranquil or more innocent.

By the time they gave up, Uncle Maurice was hoarse from shouting and from describing what he would do to Kevin if he got his hands on him. Tess's heart was in her boots as she dragged after him and into the pick-up to drive home.

\*

When they broke the news to Aunt Deirdre she lowered herself into a chair.

'They can't be far away,' she said. 'Sure, where could they be?'

'I don't know,' said Uncle Maurice. 'But the four of us have already been searching for them for hours. There's no sight nor sound of them.' He said nothing for a moment, then burst out with startling vehemence, 'Oh, God, I hate those woods!'

Tess's mind was working overtime. She looked at her watch, astonished to find that it was late afternoon. What on earth did Kevin hope to achieve with that kind of stunt? And where could they all be hiding?

Aunt Deirdre looked up, her face suddenly white with terror. 'He has kidnapped them,' she said. 'As sure as I'm sitting here, that's what has happened. The same way as in the story.'

They all knew which story she was talking about, and the realisation sent a creepy shiver down Tess's spine. Surely Kevin wouldn't do something like that. Or would he? He was going through so many changes these days. What was to say that his mind wasn't changing as rapidly as his body? Maybe he wasn't who she thought he was? Maybe money mattered too much to him, just as it did to Uncle Maurice.

'We have to call the police,' said Aunt Deirdre. 'Who knows what that terrible boy will do to them?'

Tess's spirits were so low that she found she didn't care. Maybe her aunt was right. If Kevin was going to pull stupid stunts like that, then perhaps he deserved what was coming to him. It had already occurred to her that he might take to crime. Maybe it was inevitable with someone like that? Everything Tess trusted was letting her down, and there seemed to be nothing left to believe in. But to her surprise her uncle shook his head.

'No, Deirdre,' he said. 'This isn't police business.'

'What do you mean?' she asked.

'I can't explain,' he said. 'It's to do with those woods. There's something I never told you.'

Tess was watching her uncle as he spoke but now she turned to look at her aunt. The colour was draining from her face and a kind of desperation came over her.

'But we must call the police,' she said. 'We have to get the children back!'

Again Uncle Maurice shook his head. 'It's . . .' he began, then faltered. Then he tried a different tack. 'Declan . . .' Again he couldn't, or wouldn't say what was on his mind, but the effect of the name on Aunt Deirdre was dramatic. As though she had been slapped, she jumped to her feet, her hands gripping the tea-towel that was draped over her shoulder, her knuckles tight and bloodless.

'You're mad,' she said. 'I'm calling the police.'

But Uncle Maurice, despite his obvious distress, was not beyond resorting to his usual method of getting his own way. In a sudden, red-faced rage he stood up and struck the table a massive blow with his fist.

'I won't be disobeyed in my own house,' he roared. 'If I say we don't get the police then we don't get the police! Understand?'

Aunt Deirdre looked away, but the gesture of submission wasn't enough for her husband.

'Understand?' he repeated.

Aunt Deirdre nodded, and tears of helplessness began to trickle down her nose. Tess wished she was invisible. She felt like an intruder, eavesdropping not just on a family row but on the demolition of a human spirit. She hated them both at that moment; her uncle for his cruelty, her aunt for her passive acquiescence in her own destruction. She wondered how her cousins survived the atmosphere, and was shocked back into the present when she remembered where they were, or rather, where they weren't.

Uncle Maurice was already going out again.

'Keating and his friend are leaving,' he said. 'They've already done a lot more tramping around in the woods than they bargained for.' He was outside the door and pulling it closed behind them when he paused and turned back. His tone was soft and apologetic as he said, 'I'll find them, Deirdre. Don't you worry now. I'll find them.'

As soon as he was gone, Tess realised that she had made no offer to help. There seemed no point. But her uncle's mention of Declan had given her an idea.

'I'll make you a nice cup of tea,' she said to her aunt, who stood leaning against the table as if in shock.

'You're a good girl, Tess,' she answered, straightening up and moving over to the window.

'Where does Uncle Declan live?' said Tess.

Her aunt turned slowly to face her. 'What do you know about Declan?' she asked.

'Nothing,' said Tess. 'It's just that Orla told me this morning that she'd bring me to meet him, and then Unc . . .'

But she didn't get to finish her sentence. 'That stupid girl,' said Aunt Deirdre, her voice carrying an unusual note of anger. 'She spends half her life with her head in a book and the other half with it in the clouds.'

Tess nodded, expecting more, but it seemed that her aunt had no more to say. She decided to press the matter.

'But maybe that's where they've gone?' she said. 'If he lives around there somewhere, maybe they met up with him?'

'Whisht, child,' said Aunt Deirdre. 'That's enough of that talk. Orla was wrong to be misleading you like that.'

'Why? What do you mean, misleading?'

Aunt Deirdre realised that she couldn't evade the question any longer. She sighed deeply. 'Your uncle Maurice had a brother,' she said. 'A twin brother. That's who Declan is. But the children haven't gone to see him, I promise you that.'

'Why?' said Tess.

'Because,' said Aunt Deirdre, 'he doesn't exist. Your uncle needs his head examining, and so does Orla. Maurice's brother Declan has been dead for twenty years.'

Tess went upstairs and stood at the window of Orla's room. As she looked across at the mountain, there was a horrible, empty feeling beneath her ribcage, and it had nothing to do with hunger.

Tomorrow was her birthday. Tonight she would have to decide on the form that she would take on for the rest of her life. But the world didn't seem to make sense any more. She couldn't get a proper grip on what was happening; still less on what was going to happen. It was like trying to put a jigsaw puzzle together; it ought to have been simple, but the pieces kept changing their shape whenever she looked at them. She felt sorry for herself, that all these things should get in the way of the momentous decision that was facing her. But no sooner did she feel the self-pity beginning to get a grip than she became disgusted with it. She could waste what remained to her of her powers or she could use them. At that moment, it was the only choice that she had to make. Other bridges would have to be crossed when she got to them, but for the moment she could only take one step at a time. And once she realised that, the next step became clear. There was only one way to make a proper search of the area. And there was only one person who could do it.

# CHAPTER TWELVE

Tess dropped down from the window and caught herself on jackdaw wings to fly clear of the house unnoticed. The bright little bird was fun to be, full of cocky courage; both wild and people-wise, the way the rats were. As she flew, Tess considered the jackdaw as a possible future. It would allow her to stay close to human life and to observe it from the chimneys and ruins which jackdaws chose for their nesting sites.

There were other possibilities among the bird world, as well. Swallows, perhaps, or swifts, both species forever on the wing, making great journeys across the world, following the sun. Their grace and speed, and the perfection of their aeronautic design had always appealed to Tess's aesthetic sense. She Switched now, choosing the swift for its greater size and speed, and its tendency to fly higher.

Soon she was above the woods, darting and

wheeling, peering down through the trees. There was movement down there all right, but there was nothing unusual about any of it. There were bluetits and chaffinches flitting between the branches, and rats scuttling over the mossy floor. Tess needed to get closer. A moment later she was gliding on sparrow-hawk wings to break her fall. If the swift represented nature's finest long-distance design, the sparrowhawk was her prototype for the low-flying jet plane. Barely clearing the highest branches, she skimmed above the trees, missing nothing that moved beneath them. The birds clucked and rattled and scolded, warning each other of her presence, but her hard hawk-heart despised them. Let them natter away all they liked. She had more important things on her mind.

She was close to the face of the rock when she spotted Uncle Maurice. Rising, tilting her wings at right angles to the ground, she wheeled across the sheer surface and swept in for a better look. What she saw as she overflew him for a second time puzzled her and she decided to gear down and get closer. As a wood-pigeon she dropped down among the branches and made a clattery, feather-ruffling landing, making a mental note to remove that par-ticular bird from her 'possibles' list. At least there was no harm done. The other woodland birds were well accustomed to clumsy pigeon landings, and if Uncle Maurice noticed at all, he gave no sign.

Tess cocked her head and looked down with one eye. Her uncle was standing at the foot of the crag, so close that he could have reached out and touched the bare rock where it rose from a jumble of large boulders, fallen from above. Now that she was close she could hear that he was speaking but, as alwa' when she was in animal form, Tess could not und' stand the words. She could, however, often get a sense of the mood of the speaker, and it seemed to her now that Uncle Maurice was pleading, or begging, or even praying.

But why at the rock-face? She switched again, to a robin this time. It was the only bird that would, under normal circumstances, get as close to a human being as she now wanted to be. As she dropped down to the ground, she recognised where she was. It was where the wolfhound had appeared when she had been driven into the woods by Bran and Sceolan. She had passed it several times already that day, during her searches with Uncle Maurice, and each time he had hesitated, and called extra loud and extra long. It had given Tess the creeps then and it gave her the creeps now. She puffed out her feathers and ruffled them all, then hugged them tight around herself again.

She was just about to hop closer, on to a nearby branch, when Uncle Maurice suddenly thumped the rock with his fist. It must have hurt, but he did it again anyway, and then again. The pleading tone in his voice had changed to one of anger. He kicked the rock with one foot, then the other, shouting at it, working himself into a frenzy of flailing boots and fists like a child having a tantrum.

The power of his anger was too much for the sensitive little bird. Tess hopped up through the branches and reverted to the sparrowhawk shape again to complete her aerial search of the woods.

It didn't take long. Nothing worth seeing could escape the keen eyes of the hawk. On the assumption that if Kevin and the children were not in the woods then they must have left them, Tess flew high again and began to survey the surrounding countryside in slowly widening circles.

Still there was no sign. A pair of tourists were climbing up the other side of the mountain. A few more were on bicycles pedalling slowly along a meandering back lane. The usual sparse traffic of muddy cars and tractors crawled along the narrow roads.

Tess flew higher and widened the area of search. She flew over a farmer and her dog checking cattle, and a bird-watcher who watched Tess through binoculars, tempting her to give him a display of aerobatics that he would never forget. She flew over a boy on a bicycle, heading away from the area. There was something familiar about him, and she wheeled about and flew back. She lost height to get a closer look and then, unable to believe her eyes, she dropped on to a telegraph pole and watched as the boy on the bike approached. There was no doubt about it, now. It was Kevin.

Tess dropped down behind the thick hedge and Switched back to her human self.

'Kevin!'

He nearly fell off the bike with surprise, then came to a wobbly halt.

'Here!' Tess called, trying to find a break in the hazel wide enough to climb through.

'Oh, Switch, for cripe's sake,' said Kevin. 'There's no one about.'

She did, just for a moment, slipping easily through in the shape of a stoat before emerging on to the road as a human again.

'Where are you going?' she asked. 'Where are the others?'

'What others?' asked Kevin.

89

Tess was surprised at the anger her reply revealed. 'You know perfectly well who I'm talking about!'

But Kevin was angry, too. 'I'm sick of you, Tess!' he shouted back. 'First you promise to set up a scheme for me and then you back out and drop me in it on my own. Then, when it backfires in my face, you don't even come and look for me! You just leave me to try and cope with it and carry on as though nothing had happened!'

'Oh, right,' said Tess, discovering that she was shouting as well. 'So you kidnap my cousins to get your own back!'

'I what?'

For a moment, Tess believed that Kevin's astonishment was genuine. Then she remembered what she had seen; his expression as he snubbed his nose at them the last time she saw him.

'It's a good act, Kevin,' she said. 'But it doesn't cut any ice with me. I saw you, remember? I was there when you went off with them into the woods.'

Kevin shook his head in bewilderment. 'I don't know which one of us is cracked, but I haven't got a clue what you're talking about. I haven't been anywhere near the woods since I left the rats there.'

'But I saw you!'

'No, Tess. You didn't. You couldn't have done. It must have been someone else.'

Tess shook her head. 'Where were you, then,' she said, 'if you weren't at the woods?'

'This is ridiculous,' said Kevin. 'Getting the third degree from you, of all people! But if you must know, I was back at my camp site.'

'All this time?'

'Yes, all this time. I was wondering if you were ever going to turn up!' His face coloured with embarrassment, but he went on. 'I was angry and lonely, Tess. I couldn't believe that you didn't come and see if I was all right.'

Tess sat down on a rock. Her spirit kept doing somersaults, then landing flat on its face. She wanted to believe what Kevin was saying; his friendship meant so much to her. And yet she had seen him with her own eyes. He had to be lying.

Kevin sat down beside her. 'What did you see, Tess?' he asked. 'You'd better tell me what's happening.'

Tess struggled with the idea that he was playing some awful trick on her, then gave in to trust. Feeling slightly foolish, she went through the events of the day from beginning to end. Kevin listened carefully, looking down at the ground between his feet. When she had brought him up to the present, he shook his head in bewilderment.

'I don't know what's going on,' he said. 'I can't even begin to explain it. But I can tell you one thing for certain. Whoever it was that you saw in the woods today, it wasn't me.'

'Who was it, then?' said Tess.

Kevin shrugged. 'I don't know. Your guess is as good as mine. Maybe someone who looks very like me. Maybe . . .' He stopped.

'Maybe what?'

'I don't know. But do you remember asking me once if I had noticed anything strange about those woods?'

Tess nodded and he went on, 'Well, what if there is something we haven't thought of yet? We get complacent so easily, even people like us who have seen so much. Especially us, perhaps. We think we've seen all there is to see, or been all there is to be. But maybe we haven't. Maybe there are things even we haven't imagined.'

Tess nodded, aware of the tingle of truth in her veins. She knew that he was right. There was something in those woods that she didn't understand. What was more, she didn't want to understand it. It made her much too afraid. It was easier to turn away, to keep close to Uncle Maurice, to pretend it wasn't happening. And when Kevin came even nearer to defining what it was, his words brought increasing fear along with them.

'Whatever is in those woods,' he said, 'made me think of the krools. Not because it's bad, necessarily. It might be. I don't know. But it reminded me of them because it's old. Older than we are, Tess. Older than civilisation, even.'

Tess nodded, remembering the shadows, the strange figure, the ghostly atmosphere.

'Whatever it is we're dealing with,' Kevin went on, 'it's ancient.'

# CHAPTER THIRTEEN

Tess took to the skies again to have a look around. She flew back towards the farm and spotted Uncle Maurice walking away from the woods and back across the meadows, his eyes downcast. The dogs were at his heels, equally dejected.

While Tess patrolled above, Kevin cycled back along the narrow, meandering roads and down the stony track which led to the crag. At the edge of the woods he hid his bicycle among thick stalks of hazel and, satisfied that they hadn't been spotted, Tess dropped down and joined him in human form.

Together they stood looking in among the trees. Evening was approaching and shadows were beginning to creep out from beneath the rocks and bushes. The raven flew over, looking down at them, making Tess feel exposed and vulnerable. She stepped forward and Kevin followed.

Among the branches a bird fluttered and a leaf fell.

Everything else was silent. Even though she felt much safer with Kevin beside her, Tess found that she was holding her breath. Despite the fresh, vibrant greens of the mosses and leaves, the woods were eerie. Like a stone circle or an earthwork, they had the atmosphere of a place which belonged to another age, a place where the living were somehow as insubstantial as the dead.

The two friends stayed close together as they made their way through the trees, keeping roughly parallel to the crag, calling occasionally as they went. Gradually the birds became accustomed to their presence and began to sing again, making the woods seem less forbidding. When they reached the opposite end and came out of the trees and on to the limestone pavement, Kevin sat down and shook his head.

'It doesn't make sense,' he said.

'I know,' said Tess.

'No. I mean, it doesn't make sense to search like this.'

'Why?' asked Tess.

'Because humans are the worst thing to be. You should do it, Tess. As a dog or a hawk or something.'

But Tess shook her head. 'I've already covered the place from the air. And I'm not going in there on foot. Not on my own, whatever form I'm in.' She told him about the wolfhound she had met, but found that she couldn't bring herself to mention the antlered figure, even to him. 'And in any case,' she finished, 'Uncle Maurice has just been here with Bran and Sceolan. Surely they would have found the kids if anyone could.'

Kevin sighed. 'I suppose there's no alternative, then,' he said, standing up and moving towards the woods again. 'But there doesn't seem to be much point, really, does there? I mean, if they were in there, surely they would have been found by now?'

Tess had to agree. 'But what can we do? We can't just give up on them.'

They had just entered the woods again when the sudden scuttle of a startled rat made them both stop. For a long moment Kevin stared at the spot where the worm-like tail had disappeared, and then he said, 'I can't believe we're being so stupid. Why are we wasting our time searching for the kids when there's bound to be someone here who saw where they went.'

'Of course!' said Tess. 'The rats!'

Kevin nodded. 'But I'd better leave it to you to talk to them this time. I don't think I'm in their good books.'

They moved on towards the centre of the woods, where they would have the best chance of gathering all the rats. Then, while Kevin settled himself among the trees, Tess walked a short distance away and Switched. To a human the woods appeared quiet and empty, but to a rat they were anything but. The surroundings were alive with rustlings and squabblings and a profusion of irritable images as the farm rats continued their unwilling resettlement. For a few moments the altered perceptions were disorientating, but it didn't last long. By now Tess's rat form was nearly as familiar as her human one and, since her rat mind was scarcely concerned at all with the worries that beset her as a human, Tess found it oddly comforting. She had a sudden insight into the way Kevin felt and his reasons for wishing that he had remained in rat form, but before she could dwell on it, he flashed her a reminder of her business.

'Tail Short Seven Toes having a snooze, huh?' In

his thought projection he used the name that had been given to her by the Dublin rats more than a year ago. To have a name she needed some kind of distinguishing mark, and one of the city rats had obliged her by biting off the end of her tail. Kevin sent another image; of Tess in rat form sitting in the lotus position, eyes closed.

'Tail Short Seven Toes meditating, huh?'

In return, Tess sent an image of Kevin in a huge glass of lemonade, floating around among berg-sized ice-cubes. 'Boy chill out, huh?'

But she got the message. She listened until she could hear nothing that sounded threatening, then sent out a gentle Rat invitation.

'Usguys gathering, huh? Usguys telling stories huh, huh?'

Rats are basically sensuous creatures; they love to eat and sleep and bring up their young as safely as possible. But Tess had learnt that they also love stories and often told them as a way of transmitting information about their surroundings and the world beyond. Tess had spent hour after hour telling her Switching stories to the rats at home in Dublin, and had become known as something of a star performer. But on this occasion she was eager to listen, not to tell.

The rats finished what they were doing before making their way along the network of subtle little pathways which criss-crossed the woods. They came in dribs and drabs and in no particular hurry, so the meeting had a casual air about it. Tess waited patiently, greeting the rats as they arrived, exchanging scents and names. There was an extremely awkward moment when the group of kitchen adolescents arrived, but their mother was far too busy instructing them on the rules of introduction to bother about an old argument with Tess. By the time she had disciplined them into orderly and respectful behaviour, the numbers had swelled surprisingly. Beyond the gathering a few stragglers were still arriving, but Tess decided there was no need to wait any longer. As soon as the introductions were over, she began the story-telling procedure herself by giving the gathered rats the image of the old one-toothed rat, hanging dead by his tail from Uncle Maurice's hand. A wave of sorrow passed through the assembly and there was a brief, respectful silence. Then the other rats began to tell their stories.

Tess had to work hard to hide her amusement. With minor variations, the accounts of the last two days were the same. The rats had been happy at the farm but they had believed the Big Foot who knew their language and they had followed him with fear and trembling to the woods. Everything was exaggerated, from the surprise at being woken to the promises of an idyllic haven. Tess was particularly amused by their image of Kevin, which was about as unflattering as it was possible to be. She glanced across to where he sat, in beast-learnt silence among the trees. He winked back, clearly glad that the rats didn't know he was there. They were very angry with him. No sooner had they arrived in the promised land than they had been invaded by dogs and a great many Big Feet tramping everywhere.

A human being is huge to a rat; earth-shakingly heavy and genuinely frightening. But in their telling of the day's events, the rats were outrageously magnifying the size and numbers of the searchers. Uncle Maurice and the businessmen crashed back and forth, their feet colossal and clumsy, crushing rocks and making craters in the ground. Even her own trainers appeared as killing machines, and the care she always took when walking in the countryside was distorted by the rats into purposeful malevolence. The dogs were monstrous bloodhounds with noses that vacuumed up whole litters of baby rats and blew away the carefully constructed nests of the beleaguered settlers. The images piled upon each other, exaggeration upon exaggeration, giving the impression that there was barely a square foot of the woods that had not been occupied all day by massive, tramping feet. Tess listened patiently, showing her appreciation by joining the occasional chorus of 'yup, yup,' and waiting for the excitement to run its course. When everyone had calmed down a bit, it was possible that she might get some more accurate information.

But suddenly an absurd image entered the babble. The pictures of huge, stomping boots were being repeated again and again, almost like a drumbeat or a chant. But thrown in among the big feet, like the tinkling of a little bell, was a tiny pair of red ones.

Tess focused as hard as she could, waiting for the stray image to return and hoping to identify the rat that had produced it. Sure enough it came again, bright and ridiculous among the almost military drabness. The picture was coming from somewhere on the left-hand side of the crowd, and the third time it was sent, Tess zoned in.

The rat who had seen the red wellies was fully grown but very small compared to the rest of the fat, meal-fed rats. There was something odd about her as well; she was sitting on her haunches and nodding fervently, like some religious zealot of the rodent world. With a faint shock, Tess realised that she had seen her before, and at the same time she remembered where. She had met her in the hall-way on her first visit to the rat world beneath the farm, and she had flashed her that strange, poetic welcome. She had forgotten it at the time because of the argument in the kitchen, but now that she thought about it she began to wonder whether the rat who had sent it was the full shilling. If not, the sighting of the red wellies might prove to be unreliable.

The story of the Big Feet was still continuing. While she waited for it to come to an end, Tess glanced over at Kevin again. But this time he was not looking towards her but away, at something deeper in the woods. For a reason that she didn't understand, the sight gave Tess the creeps.

She turned back to the gathering and joined the chorus of 'yup, yups' that greeted the end of the story. The protocol of such occasions required that she, as the visitor, now tell another one, but as politely as she could she declined the honour and, in the general melee that followed, she made her way over to the strange, dissenting rat.

As Tess approached she nodded again, so deeply that it was more like a bow.

'Cat Friend,' she said, her images fresh and clear.

'Tail Short Seven Toes,' Tess replied and, wasting no time on ceremony, continued, 'Little red wellies, huh? Huh?'

Cat Friend was delighted to cooperate. 'Yup, yup,' she said, and flashed again the image of Colm's red boots.

'More feet, huh?' said Tess, offering various feet-images but purposefully avoiding any that might prompt Cat Friend into an untruthful answer. If she was a little uncertain about her facts, she might now be tricked into giving herself away.

But Tess needn't have worried. Cat Friend's next image was clear beyond any shadow of doubt. There were four pairs of feet; three small and one big. Apart from the red wellies there were Orla's boots, and Brian's and, to Tess's surprise, a pair of very familiar trainers.

'Huh? Huh?' she said, needing to see them again, needing to be sure.

Cat Friend repeated obligingly. There was no doubt about it. The trainers were Kevin's.

Tess sat up on her haunches and turned to look at him, but the spot where he had been was empty. She craned her neck, then jumped up on to a rock for a better view. Between the trees she caught a glimpse of him, moving swiftly away, almost out of sight already. Unwilling to frighten the rats she raced after him on foot for a few yards before Switching into a pigeon and dodging among the trees in wild pursuit.

But it was already too late. There was no sign of him. It was impossible, but it was true. She had seen him only a moment ago, but now he was nowhere. She flew until she met the crag, then flew back, quartering the area in one direction and then the other. She flew until her own panic exhausted her pigeon wings, and then she came to a quivering halt on a dead branch lodged between two trees. It couldn't have happened. He had to be there.

She dropped down to the ground and Switched back to human form, her limbs still trembling from fear and fatigue. The rats were gone, vanished back beneath the rocks and roots and leaves. Once again, Tess was alone in the woods.

'Kevin?' she called.

There was no answer.

'Kevin! I know you're there!'

In the pause that followed, a faint breeze sighed among the branches. It seemed to carry words.

'Come on, Tess. Come with me.'

Fear grasped her like a claw and, without knowing where or from what, she began to run. As though it had somehow succeeded in its aim, the voice came again, whispering through the trees.

But this time, it was laughing.

# CHAPTER FOURTEEN

Tess's fear and disappointment made her reckless. In the form of a jackdaw she tore back to her open window and, without even bothering to check that the coast was clear, she flung herself inside. Before she hit the bed she Switched, and along with her human form came all its attendant miseries. Maybe Kevin was right. Maybe a rat was the best thing to be.

And maybe he wasn't right. Maybe he had always been the scurrilous, criminal-minded truant that she had believed him to be when she first met him, all that time ago during the freak winter. Perhaps she was wrong to have ever trusted him, or to have rescued him when, in phoenix form, he was trapped in the zoo. She wanted so badly to believe that he was innocent; that he had nothing to do with the kidnap of the children; above all that he hadn't lied to her. But all the evidence suggested otherwise.

Emotionally she was numb, too exhausted by the ups and downs of the day to feel anything any more. But her body still had needs. Much as she dreaded an encounter with her distressed aunt, Tess knew that she would have to get something to eat. The ordinariness of it was comforting, but as she crossed to the door of the bedroom her eye fell on the book that Orla had been reading, lying open on its face, the deer-man gazing up from the cover. Whatever it was that she was mixed up in, it wasn't over yet.

As she had expected, her aunt was in the kitchen, sitting at the table as though she hadn't moved all day.

'Where on earth have you been, child?' she said.

'Nowhere. Why?'

'You were gone. I didn't hear you come in. How did you come in without me hearing you?'

'You were dozing, probably,' said Uncle Maurice. He was standing by the back door, leaning against the wall so quietly that Tess hadn't noticed he was there. His face was grey and deeply lined, as though he had aged ten years in the last few hours.

'At least we have one of them,' said Aunt Deirdre. 'God forbid that we should lose my sister's child as well as our own.'

She was glaring at Uncle Maurice as she spoke, and then, as though Tess's presence had made her brave, she burst out, 'Please, Maurice. Please let's get the police in on this.'

Tess had been edging towards the bread-bin, but the anguish in her aunt's voice brought her to a standstill.

'Tell him, Tess,' she went on. 'Make him see sense. What's past is past, we know nothing of that. But what is happening here is a kidnap, isn't it? Surely you can see that? We need to call the police!'

Tess looked from her aunt to her uncle and back again. She had no idea what the reference to the past was about, but it was clear that Deirdre and Maurice understood each other perfectly.

'I've told you a hundred times, Deirdre,' said Uncle Maurice. 'The police can do no good here. They'd only be wasting their time, just like before.'

'Before?' said Tess. 'What do you mean, "before"?'

Aunt Deirdre shook her head, and there was a horrified expression on her face. 'You're mad, Maurice,' she said. 'I never thought the day would come when I'd hear myself say it. I always denied it, always. Even when others said it I refused to listen. But I believe them now, all right.'

A glimmer of fear crossed Aunt Deirdre's features as she spoke, but for once it was unfounded. Uncle Maurice had no anger left in him.

'They'll be home,' he said. 'Wait till you see.' And before she could answer, he stepped out through the door and walked away across the yard.

Aunt Deirdre stared at the place where he had been.

'What did you mean?' Tess asked. 'About the past.'

'Hush, child,' said Aunt Deirdre. 'Don't be worrying. Get yourself a bite to eat, there. You must be starved.'

Tess didn't need to be asked twice, but nor was she so easily put off track.

'Do other people really say that Uncle Maurice is mad?' she asked.

'That's enough about that, now,' said her aunt.

Tess pressed on. 'But why? Why would they say he was mad?'

Aunt Deirdre sighed deeply and then, as though her resistance had finally given way, the words began to pour out of her.

'I wouldn't have told you, child, but I can't see the harm in it now, to tell the truth. There was an awful tragedy here, you see. Awful.'

The hairs on Tess's neck stood up, but she buttered bread calmly, willing her aunt to continue. She did.

'Your uncle had a twin brother. Declan was his name, and it's said that the two of them were so close that you rarely saw daylight between them. But Declan died, as I told you earlier.'

'How?' said Tess.

'That's the mystery,' said Aunt Deirdre. 'No one knows. He disappeared in the early hours of one morning and no trace was ever found of him.'

'They didn't find his body?'

'No. Nothing.'

'Then how do they know he died?'

'There was no other explanation,' said Aunt Deirdre. 'A boy can't just vanish into thin air, now, can he?'

Tess nodded in agreement.

'Where?' she said. 'Where did he disappear?'

'No one knows, for sure. All we know is that Maurice believed that he was in those woods, and for weeks afterwards he had to be carried out of them at night, otherwise he would never have left them at all. Calling his brother's name, he was. Convinced that Declan was in there and would come out.'

Aunt Deirdre stood up and moved around in an agitated way, putting on the kettle and emptying the teapot into the sink.

'There were even some who said . . .' she stopped and stared at Tess vacantly, and it was as though her anxiety had brought her to the brink of madness as well.

'What did they say?' Tess asked, but Aunt Deirdre shook her head and turned to look out of the window, in the direction of the mountain. It was clear that she had said as much as she was going to.

But it didn't make sense. Why had Orla said that she would take Tess to meet Uncle Declan? How could she meet someone who was dead? And where did Kevin fit into the picture?

Tess found cheese in the fridge and made sandwiches, then took them up to her room. Far from making things clearer, her aunt's words had only made the mystery deeper and more frightening. It was almost as though history was repeating itself, with Uncle Maurice's own children vanishing in the same way that his brother had. But if that was the case, why would he be so reluctant to call in the police? And who was it that whispered to her in the woods?

She sat on the bed and ate the sandwiches without enthusiasm. Afterwards, tired and dispirited, she threw herself on to the bed. Every mystery had a simple explanation, she knew that, and she was fed up of being thwarted in everything she tried to do. Miserably, she rolled on to her side and curled up like a baby.

She thought of the land again, the fresh, green beauty of the woods and the greed of the people who wanted to destroy it in order to line their own pockets. She didn't want to be an adult in a society like that, where no one cared about anything except money. She envisioned the world as a grey, barren place, where nothing lived except human beings and nothing grew except the food they ate. Like a plague on the earth; like locusts they destroyed everything before them, like locusts they could see no further than their own, immediate greed.

She wouldn't join them. Better to be an animal, even a greedy one like a pig or a rat. At least they didn't pretend to care. People were worse. People were hypocrites. A few tears ran down her nose and dripped on to the pillow.

Thoughts of Lizzie returned. If only she could see the old woman. She was sure that Lizzie would have the answer. She always did. But Lizzie lived two hundred miles away, and Tess couldn't think of any way of getting to her in time.

Her mind ran back over their last conversation. What was it that Lizzie had said? Something about ancestors.

Ancestors?

Despite the seriousness of the situation, Tess laughed, struck by the image of old men in medieval attire roaming round in the landscape.

'Lizzie sends her regards,' she said to the empty room.

A sudden gust of wind rattled the window hard, and Tess flinched. There was something else that the old woman had said. What was it? Tess concentrated and, obligingly, the words came to her.

'Does we believe what we sees, or does we see what we believe?'

Across the fields, at the foot of the mountain, something was happening that she didn't understand. She stood up to go to the window, but her eye fell on Orla's book. *Story or History?* What did it mean? Idly, Tess reached out and picked it up, wondering if there was anything in its pages that might give her a clue. But when she saw what was lying beneath it, she gave up all thoughts of reading.

It was Orla's inhaler.

Tess knew now that the chips were down. She could still cop out, of course; give her aunt the inhaler and let her worry about what was happening to Orla out there in the woods with the evening drawing in. She could stay here in her room with the light on and eat sandwiches and worry about her future. But if she did any of those things it would be an admission that her fear had defeated her. And suddenly she realised that she didn't need Lizzie to tell her what to do. The truth, plain and simple, was that if anyone had a chance of finding those children it was her. What could she possibly encounter, after all, worse than the bone-chilling krools or the terrible vampire that Martin had learnt to become?

When the sun rose the next morning her powers would be gone. The events of the day were moving too fast, robbing her of time and space to think, and it looked now as though she wasn't going to have time to make a considered choice about what to be. But perhaps it didn't matter. Perhaps it didn't help to have time to think. Up until now all the thinking in the world hadn't helped her to arrive at a decision.

She slipped the inhaler into her pocket and moved towards the window. For the moment, at least, none of it mattered. For the next few hours she still had her Switching powers. If she did not use them while she could, she might spend the rest of her life regretting it.

With a feeling of courage returning, of becoming herself again after a long absence, Tess flung open the window.

# CHAPTER FIFTEEN

Tess had thought that her Uncle Maurice had set out for the crag, but as she flew out of her bedroom window, in jackdaw shape again, she spotted him beneath her, letting in the cows to be milked. She was relieved. It would give her a bit more freedom in the woods.

As she flew, she thought about what she needed to do, and by the time she reached the woods she had worked out what her first step would be. She dropped down through the trees near where she had last seen Kevin, then Switched into rat form. She had some information to gather and, as soon as she had adjusted and checked the environment for safety, she gave out a call in Rat. But this time she wasn't summoning a gathering. She was looking for Cat Friend.

It wasn't long before she arrived; puzzled but cooperative. Tess realised that she liked this strange little rat despite, or maybe because of, her idiosyncratic behaviour. And it seemed, by the affectionate way that Cat Friend touched noses, that she felt the same way. Tess felt a wash of sadness as the thought came to her that she would soon be leaving the animal world for ever. No sooner had the thought arrived, however, than another superseded it. Why should she think like that? She hadn't made her mind up. Perhaps she would stay a rat, be a rat forever, living and dying alongside Cat Friend and the others. Why not?

But there was other business to take care of first. Cat Friend had told her that she had seen Kevin and the children in the woods earlier that day. Now Tess wanted to know if she had seen where they had gone.

'Yup, yup,' said Cat Friend, nodding like a car toy again; full of certainty. 'Cat Friend watching Small Big Feet. Cat Friend following.'

Tess was delighted. 'Wise Cat Friend,' she said. 'Cat Friend following into the woods, huh? Out of the woods, huh? Huh?'

But the image that Cat Friend returned in answer shook Tess's confidence in her severely. It showed the people involved as clearly as ever; Kevin leading and the other three following closely behind. But where they went was quite impossible. According to Cat Friend, they walked right through the solid face of the crag and disappeared.

It didn't seem to surprise her at all that four humans should do such a thing. But it didn't fit into Tess's interpretation of reality.

'Nananana!' she said. 'Small Big Feet bumping into the rock, falling over backwards. Small Big Feet walking into the crag and hurting themselves.'

Cat Friend was offended by Tess's attitude and puffed out her coat and turned her face away. Tess tried to repair the damage, explaining about doors and how they worked, but Cat Friend was adamant. She had been there. She had seen what happened. Over and over again she repeated the image of what she had seen. The four people had walked up to the rock-face and vanished into it.

Tess didn't know what to do. If there had been any other leads at all she might have forgotten about Cat Friend and her rambling mind. Since there weren't, she did the only thing that presented itself to her. She asked Cat Friend to show her the place where it had happened.

The other rat came out of her sulk instantly and skipped on ahead energetically. Occasionally she hung back and waited for Tess to catch up, touching her nose delightedly before bounding on across the rocks again. As she followed, Tess found herself wondering if the whole world hadn't gone mad around her, or whether it was she herself who was mad. It wasn't until they came near to their destination that she realised there had to be some truth in what Cat Friend was saying. Because it was the place that, somehow, she had been led to every time she had gone into those woods. It was the place where she had seen the strange wolfhound, and where Kevin had been when she last saw him yesterday. There was no doubt about it; there had to be a secret door of some kind. Cat Friend was probably right about that. It was just her way of seeing it and explaining it that was odd.

She stood back now and watched as Tess scuttled along the base of the rock, standing on her hind legs from time to time and stretching up with her front paws, trying to find some clue to where the entrance might be. There was nothing, though, and when she had exhausted all the possibilities that her rat mind could conceive of, she realised that she needed to be human again.

There is no way to apologise in Rat, but Tess was truly sorry for what she did next. Because when Cat Friend saw Tail Short Seven Toes disappear and a rather large Small Big Foot appear out of nowhere, she got the fright of her life. In a sudden, furry flash she was gone, out of sight beneath the nearest rock. Tess hoped that she wasn't too badly shocked, and that she would see her again.

But there were other, more urgent matters on her mind. She walked back and forth along the base of the crag and then, seeing no obvious signs of a door of any kind, prepared herself for a long, meticulous search. Yard by yard and inch by inch she examined the face of the rock, prising at every crack and fault, poking into every overhang and shadow. When she had covered the whole area and a good distance either side she went back again with a stone, knocking the rock at intervals and listening for hollow resonances. But no matter how hard she tried or how careful she was, she could find no sign of an entrance of any kind. Eventually, tired and despondent, she hurled her sounding stone far out into the trees and sank to the ground.

It was beginning to get dark. Already the moon was rising and trying to peer in among the trees. Whatever chance she had of finding her cousins seemed to be fading fast. Every fibre of Tess's being screamed against the sheer frustration of it. First she believed that there was a door, that there had to be to explain the mysterious appearances and disappearances in the area. Then she was equally certain that there wasn't a door, not now or ever. And as she swung wildly between these two conflicting certainties, she became aware that she was being watched. Not far away, on a moss-coated boulder that was just about level with Tess's eyes, a brown rat was sitting.

'Cat Friend?' she called.

'Yup, yup,' said Cat Friend, scrambling down from her perch and approaching along the ground until she was close to Tess's outstretched leg. Tess shook her head in surprise. In all the years that she had been using her powers to Switch she had never known an animal to make a connection between her human form and her animal ones. Not even Algernon, her pet white rat, had ever realised that the brown cousin that regularly visited him in the evenings was actually her. But there was no doubt now that Cat Friend understood.

'Tail Short Seven Toes, huh? Huh?' she asked, giving the clear image of Tess's rat form and then an image of her Switching to human form which was so accurate it made Tess tingle all over.

'Yup, yup,' said Tess. 'Cat Friend watching, huh? Cat Friend not afraid?'

The little rat shook her coat then tightened it so that she looked her sleek, proud best.

'Cat Friend watching,' she said. And then, in a series of images so clear that they had to be truth, she showed Tess that she was not the first Switcher she had come across. To Tess's growing amazement, her new friend revealed that the white cat in the farmyard, the one whose friendship had given her the name, was itself a Switcher. The images followed, one upon the other; the white cat becoming a stoat, a hare, a raven. Nor were the descriptions anywhere near an end when Cat Friend, quite abruptly, sent an urgent image of rats fleeing from danger, then turned on her heel and vanished among a cluster of nearby tree-roots.

Instinctively, Tess leapt to her feet and turned to see what it was that had frightened her little friend. Not more than a few feet away, leaning against the sheer face of the crag, was Kevin.

He smiled. 'Hi, Tess,' he said.

'How . . . But how did you get there?' Tess replied.

'Easy,' he said. 'I just crept up on you.'

'I don't think so,' said Tess, realising that her frustration was rapidly turning into anger. 'Or at least, you might have crept up on me, but you would never have been able to creep up on her.'

She pointed at the roots of the tree where Cat Friend had disappeared. Kevin laughed.

'Good thinking,' he said.

'So where did you appear from?' Tess asked. 'And what have you done with my cousins?'

'I haven't done anything with your cousins,' said Kevin. 'It's not my fault if they followed me, is it?'

'Followed you where?'

'In there, of course.' He pointed to the bare rock. 'Where else?'

'Show me, then,' said Tess. 'I'm fed up of searching and getting nowhere. If there's a door, where is it?'

'I can't show you what you're not able to see,' said Kevin. 'But perhaps if you follow me I can lead you in.'

With that he Switched into a barn owl and, with a brief swish of heavy wings, he flew up through the trees.

Tess stared after the bird, ghostly pale against the night sky. Despite the evidence of her eyes, she was unable to believe what she had just seen. All the laws of her world, every last one of them, seemed to have been turned on their heads. Kevin could not Switch. He had passed fifteen and, as all Switchers must, he had lost the ability. And yet she could not doubt that she had just seen it happen.

Already the owl was out of sight above the trees. Tess found that she was rooted to the spot, and couldn't follow. But Kevin wasn't about to leave without her and soon returned, Switching back to human form again.

'But you can't, Kevin!' said Tess. 'It's impossible!'

'Come with me, Tess,' he said. The words and the way he said them rang a bell in her mind, but before she could remember why he spoke again.

'Come on. Let me show you what's possible and what isn't. Let me show you what you could be, Tess. Before it's too late.'

And with that he was an owl again, lifting towards the skies. This time, Tess followed.

It was exhilarating to be up there, with eyes that pierced the darkness and wings as silent as the watching moon. Beneath them as they flew, the woodland creatures clung to their shadows and waited for their pale enemies to pass over. Tess followed compliantly as the owl that had been Kevin spiralled higher and higher. The lights of the house became visible, and so did the dejected figure of Uncle Maurice, crossing the fields yet again on his way to search for the children.

Higher still the two birds rose, until they were above the level of the crag and looking down on to its plateau-like summit, where the moonlight threw shadows from heaps and jumbles and circles of stone which were almost as ancient as the mountain itself. Beyond that the grey, fluid shapes of the Burren range stretched away to the edges of vision.

Tess was so entranced by the surroundings that she missed the exact moment when the other owl began to drop down out of the skies again. She followed at a distance, and he waited for her, swooping up again, then falling past her, almost drawing her into his wake. This time she kept up, reminded of another time, long ago, when she had followed Kevin in an electrifying dive into a building in Dublin. He had been a different kind of owl on that occasion and both of them had been different people. It seemed like an eternity had passed since then.

Faster and faster they fell until the thick canopy of the trees was racing up to meet them. Without hesitating, the other owl plunged straight through the leaves and, holding her breath, Tess followed. What came next happened in the blink of an eye, but there was somehow time for a thousand thoughts to flash through Tess's mind.

They entered the woods close to the crag, and the instant that Kevin was beneath the trees he levelled up and flew at breakneck speed straight towards the rock. A shock-wave passed through Tess's body, and at the same time she began to flap madly, trying to slow down and change direction at the same time. It seemed that Kevin was certain to be killed, but he wasn't. If Tess hadn't seen it with her own eyes, she would never have believed it.

Without slowing, without changing direction, he continued to fly straight towards the rock-face. But just when the bone-crunching collision seemed inevitable, he vanished. There was no doubt at all about what had happened. The owl that was Kevin hadn't Switched, nor had it become invisible. It had simply flown straight through the solid face of the rock.

# CHAPTER SIXTEEN

Despite her best efforts, Tess couldn't reduce speed fast enough. Her left wing glanced against the rock and she tumbled down the last few feet of its face like a fluttering Catherine wheel. At the bottom she picked herself up and shook her feathers, then Switched into her human frame.

Her left arm was sore and she knew by the feel of her hips and shoulders that she would have a few bruises tomorrow to show for that fall. But on what kind of body she still couldn't imagine. Tomorrow was a blank in her mental map.

And today was a disaster. She slumped to the ground and sat with her back against the rock, ignoring the damp which was beginning to soak from the mossy ground into her jeans. She found that she was no longer afraid, but she was angry. Angry at Kevin for playing tricks on her. Angry at Lizzie for talking in riddles. Angry at herself for failing to gain entrance to the rock. Even as the thought came to her, she understood why it was that she had failed. There had been an instant, she remembered, immediately after the other owl's disappearance, when she could have followed it. In that instant she had known that the key to the door in the rock was not a thing that she could find or touch, nor was it a puzzle that she could work out with her mind. The only things that could get her through were faith and courage; the ability to let go and allow herself to be governed by another reality; one that she did not understand. In that brief moment she had known all that, and she had chickened out. That was why she was still there, all alone on the outside; the one who had failed. The one left behind.

Lizzie's words returned to her again. What did she mean by believing what we see or seeing what we believe? She was certain that the words had some bearing on her situation, but she didn't know exactly how. Tess stood up and looked at the rock, but she knew in her heart that it was already too late. She had missed the moment of truth and she couldn't recreate it. She could hear her uncle's arrival at the edge of the woods; the snap of a broken branch, a whispered call.

Tess no longer knew what to believe. Somehow she had entered another world, where things weren't as they seemed, and where the rules she had come to have faith in didn't seem to apply. She wanted to believe in it. She just didn't know how.

But someone else did. The touch on her ankle was so soft that she thought a moth had brushed her and she leant down to scratch the itch. But it wasn't a moth.

'Tail Short Seven Toes sad, huh? Huh?'

Cat Friend was standing on her hind legs, clutching on to Tess's jeans with her front paw.

Tess couldn't help smiling despite her dejected mood. 'Yup, yup,' she said. 'Tail Short Seven Toes trying to get into the rock. Left all alone and sad.'

'Cat Friend helping,' said the little rat. 'Cat Friend leading Tail Short Seven Toes into the rock.'

The images were perfectly clear and Tess's spirits soared. She knew that it could work. There was no doubt at all about Cat Friend's belief and Tess felt sure that it could bolster her own sufficiently to cross the subtle barrier. But they would have to be quick. From among the trees came the sound of a grunt and a mild curse as Uncle Maurice lost his footing. He was almost there.

Tess Switched into rat form and, although Cat Friend jumped at the abruptness of the change, she didn't falter. A moment later they were scurrying towards the rock. At Cat Friend's suggestion, Tess took hold of her tail and closed her eyes. And as they began to move forward, she called on all the courage that she had ever had.

It seemed to take forever to get there. Tess waited for a resistance of some kind, or a shift in the atmosphere like the one that she experienced every time she Switched. But it didn't happen, and after a while Tess began to think that Cat Friend must be making a fool of her. But when she opened her eyes she was amazed to find that she was inside the hill and, judging by the distance they had covered, had been for some time.

She let go of Cat Friend's tail and stopped to look around. They were in a long, dimly-lit hall like a broad tunnel, lined with rough stones from the base of the walls to the crude arch high above their heads.

To a rat the place was enormous, but Tess guessed that the roof would not have been much higher than a man's head. She wondered vaguely who would have built such a place, but more perplexing was that still there was no sign of Kevin or the children.

Cat Friend seemed equally perplexed, and the two rats conferred briefly before moving on across the stony floor. At the end of the hall a stone wall blocked their way, but on the left, low down, was a hole in the wall. Although it was huge for a rat, it was small for a human. A child might have crawled through, but an adult would have had to lie down on their belly to squeeze in. Since there was no other way forward, the rats went in, all their senses straining for any signs of danger.

Before they had gone more than a few feet along this smaller tunnel, they heard sounds of life ahead, and their way was lit by a strange, golden light. A moment later they emerged into a second hall. It was roughly the same size and shape as the one they had just come through, but there all similarity ended.

For this hall was, without doubt, a fairy *sidhe*. The mysterious light that they had encountered flooded the enclosed space, but there were no lamps nor was there any opening to the outside. Tess and Cat Friend crouched at the end of the small tunnel, trying to get their bearings in the extraordinary surroundings.

The first thing Tess noticed was Orla and Brian, who were standing nearby and were involved in what appeared to be a rather cruel game. They had a small, black kitten, and they were tossing it between them as though it was a ball. Beyond them was a table, covered with the most scrumptious food that Tess had ever seen and, further on still, she could see

Kevin sitting on a pile of silken cushions, looking sulky.

Tess touched noses with Cat Friend and was about to move forward when she felt a large hand grasp her tail and lift her from the ground. Quicker than thought, she twisted in the air, in an attempt to bite the aggressor, but before her teeth reached their target the hand jerked away and she found herself being flung through the air in a wide arc.

Before she began to descend she Switched into a bat and flew on up towards the ceiling, where she gripped a rough edge of stone with her paws and waited to get her bearings. Beneath her the game had abruptly ended and Orla was clutching the kitten, which clung to her jumper with tiny claws. Beyond them Kevin was on his feet, and they were all staring towards a boy who stood beside the crawl-hole.

He, in turn, was gazing up at her. He appeared to be a teenager, around her own age. His eyes were grey and he had fair hair, but beyond that it was hard to describe him in terms of the human race. He was dressed in clothes that glimmered and moved like molten silver and gold, and his skin shone with the same, golden light that suffused the *sidhe* so that it was difficult to say whether he reflected the light or created it. But despite his extraordinary appearance, there was something about his face that was familiar to Tess. She was still racking her brains, trying to work out what it was, when he began to speak.

To her bat-brain the sound was meaningless; a booming resonance bouncing around the confined space. Intrigued, she dropped from the ceiling and fluttered to the floor beside the table, where she Switched into human form.

'Yay! Here's Tess!' Orla shouted.

'Yahoo!' yelled Brian. 'What took you so long, eh?'

Orla tossed the little black kitten towards her. As she caught it, it transformed itself into Colm, red wellies and all. Tess was so surprised by the sudden change in weight that she dropped him, but he changed into a huge, brightly-coloured butterfly as he fell, and went fluttering off around the hall.

Tess laughed, delightedly. It was like a dream come true, being among friends, all Switchers, with no one to keep secrets from. And when she perused the loaded table, she knew that she was really in heaven. All her favourite foods were there; macaroni cheese and sausages and heaps of chips with vinegar and tomato ketchup, and trifles and cream buns and too many things to take in. She reached for a chip and was about to put it in her mouth when Kevin roared from the other end of the hall.

'No, Tess! Don't eat it!'

She turned and stared at him, dumbstruck. He ran over.

'Don't eat it, Tess,' he said again. 'Don't eat anything, you hear? Nothing at all.'

From the opposite end of the hall, the strange boy advanced, speaking as he came.

'Don't listen to him, Tess. He has some very strange ideas. I can't imagine where he got them from.'

The boy was so handsome and had such an ethereal quality that Tess found it hard to disbelieve him.

'Take some, go on. Help yourself.'

But Kevin was determined. 'No, Tess. Please listen. You know it yourself, if only you'll stop and think.'

'Think about what?' asked Tess, her irritation

growing. She was remembering Kevin's deceitfulness earlier, and was not inclined to give him the benefit of the doubt. But her dilemma was shelved for the time being by a new turn of events.

Brian stepped forward and, as proud as punch, stood between Tess and the radiant boy.

'In any case,' he said, 'we are forgetting ourselves. I think we all know who you are, Tess. But I don't think you have met our Uncle Declan.'

# CHAPTER SEVENTEEN

Tess took several steps backwards, not because there was anything threatening about Declan's manner, but because she was afraid that if she took the offered hand it might not feel like flesh. Kevin moved over to her, protectively she thought, but it didn't stop the blood draining from her face, and for a moment or two she was light-headed and faint.

Declan smiled at her reaction.

'What's wrong?' he said. 'You look as if you've seen a ghost.'

'And haven't I?' said Tess.

He laughed. 'I can understand why you should think that,' he said.

The butterfly came flitting over and landed on Tess's shoulder. This time she was ready for the change, and she hefted Colm down on to her hip as he Switched.

'Go home, Tess?' he asked.

'Of course we will, Colm. I'll bring you home soon.'

But Kevin shook his head. 'You can't, Tess,' he said. 'He won't let them.'

'How can he stop them?' she said. 'Will somebody please explain to me what's going on?'

Colm wriggled to the ground and headed towards the table.

'Don't eat anything, now,' said Orla.

'Wanna sausage,' said Colm, reaching for one.

'Why can't he have one?' asked Tess.

'Because he'll have to stay here for ever if he eats anything,' said Brian.

'He's right,' said Kevin. 'Don't you remember the rules?'

'What rules? The rules of what?'

'Of places like this,' said Kevin. 'About not eating the food, no matter how delicious it looks.'

Orla had succeeded in prising the sausage out of Colm's hand, and was standing between him and the table, warding off the well-aimed blows that he was raining upon her.

'But that's ridiculous,' said Tess. 'That's just stuff out of fairy stories.'

Her words met with silence, and as she looked around the hall, she discovered that every eye in the place was turned to her, as though she was an idiot; the last one to get some glaringly obvious joke.

'It's ridiculous!' she said. 'You can't be for real.'

Still everyone stared, until she went on. 'This is the twentieth century, for cripe's sake! You're not trying to tell me there's such a thing as fairies!'

The silence that met her words was her answer. She shook her head incredulously.

'Where are they, then? These fairies?'

All the others turned their eyes towards Declan.

'But he's not a fairy!' said Tess. 'Fairies are little people who flit around in the woods and play tricks on . . .' She stopped, remembering some of her recent experiences. ' . . . and they're small,' she finished, lamely.

Declan laughed; a clear, birdlike sound that echoed throughout the long chamber.

'They're small except for the big ones,' he said.

'And they're big except for the green ones,' said Orla.

'And they're green except for the pink ones,' said Brian. 'And they all have wings except for the ones without them!'

The hall rang with laughter, and Tess would have felt left out; like a new girl at school all over again, if it hadn't been for Kevin. He wasn't laughing, and he took another protective step towards her.

But she hadn't forgotten his deceit. 'I don't know how you can be so stuck on the rules anyway,' she said, glaring at him. 'Since you seem to be able to break them when it suits you.'

'What rules?' said Kevin. 'What rule did I break?'

'Only the one that says you can't Switch any more after you're fifteen!'

Kevin shook his head in bewilderment. Colm came back and slipped a sweaty hand into hers.

'Go home, now?' he asked.

'Soon, Colm. Soon.'

She turned back to the others, and as she did so the blood left her brain again and she had to lean against the wall for support.

For there were two Kevins, identical in all respects.

The one beside her, the real Kevin, went pale and turned away. The other one laughed, and, just for an instant, the shadow that he cast upon the wall behind him grew about three feet taller and sprouted antlers. Tess took a step back, but before she could take any more drastic action the looming figure shrank and the second Kevin became Declan again.

For a long moment, everyone was too stunned to speak. But eventually Kevin found his voice. 'So that explains it,' he said. 'That's how you saw me in the woods. Except that it wasn't me at all. It was him.'

'But which one was him?' said Tess.

'The one who took the kids,' said Kevin. 'The other one was me. The one on the bicycle.'

'So how did you get in here?' Tess asked.

'Declan invited me in,' he said.

Declan nodded. 'People can't see the door because of an illusion; fairy glamour, it's called. But we can take it off if we choose to. If there's someone we want to let in.'

Tess felt hurt. 'Why didn't you take it off for me, then?' she asked.

To her disgust, Declan roared with laughter. 'I wanted to see if you could find your own way in,' he said. 'And besides, it was fun watching you wearing your brains out trying to understand what was going on.'

He laughed again and Tess decided to ignore him. She turned back to Kevin. 'Why didn't you come out, then?' she asked. 'Since you seem to be especially privileged around here.'

'Would you have, Tess?' said Kevin, looking towards the three children. 'Would you have left them here with him?'

Tess's heart seemed complete again. Whatever else might happen, she was reassured. This was the Kevin she knew and trusted.

If little Colm understood the conversation, he showed no interest in it. He tugged at Tess's hand and, when she didn't respond, he let go of it.

'Go home now!' he whined, and set off for the hole at the entrance to the hall.

He was small enough to crawl through easily. At least, in his own shape, he was. But as he dropped towards his hands and knees to go through, he turned into a pig. A large pig. Far too large to go through the hole.

Declan snickered, and despite herself Tess laughed as well.

'Why doesn't he try something smaller?' she said.

'Because it isn't him that's doing it,' said Kevin. 'It's Declan.'

Declan smiled and gave a mock bow. 'A simple enchantment,' he said.

'But how?' said Tess. 'I don't understand.' She turned to Declan. 'Who are you, anyway?'

'You know who I am,' said Declan. He nodded towards her cousins. 'I'm Maurice's brother; their uncle.'

'But you can't be. You're too young.'

Declan shook his head. 'I just look young,' he said. 'I'm what you could be, and your cousins. And what he could have been if he'd had the sense, poor soul.'

'Don't "poor soul" me!' said Kevin. 'I don't need your pity!'

'Maybe not,' said Declan. 'But I bet you'd change places with me if you could. Don't you think so, Tess?'

Tess suspected he might be right, but in deference to Kevin's feelings she said nothing.

'I did what you all wish you could do,' Declan went

on. 'I didn't give up the gift when I turned fifteen. I kept it.'

'But you can't!' said Tess. 'You have to . . .'

Declan interrupted her. 'You have to blah blah blah,' he said. 'You have to nothing. We discovered something, your uncle and I.'

'Uncle Maurice?'

'Who else? Shall I show you, Tess? Shall I show you what Maurice and I discovered in these woods?'

Tess hesitated, remembering the weird things she had seen and the fear she had experienced. What was happening here still frightened her.

'I'm not going anywhere,' she said. 'Not until I understand what's going on here. Will someone please explain?'

As soon as Colm stopped trying to get out of the crawl-hole he was relieved of his pig shape. To keep him occupied, Brian Switched into C3PO, and in immediate response, Colm turned into R2D2. Tess was satisfied as another mystery was explained, but she couldn't help wishing that she had thought of it herself, and tried it. The two metal men went to the far end of the hall, where Brian responded to his brother's bleeps and whirs in soft, patient tones.

Meanwhile, the others flopped around on the silken cushions and listened as Declan told his story.

'Maurice was the first to discover that we could change ourselves into other things,' he began.

'You mean Uncle Maurice was a Switcher, too?' said Tess.

'Is that what you call us?' said Declan. 'Switchers?'

Tess nodded, still trying to absorb the unlikely information.

'It isn't the word I would have used,' said Declan, 'but I suppose it doesn't matter. He was the first of us to discover it, and for a long time I was afraid, and wouldn't join him when he came out here to play with the Good People.'

'The Good People,' said Tess. 'You mentioned them before, Orla, didn't you?'

'Fairies,' said Orla. 'It's what people called them in the old days.'

'That's right,' said Declan. 'And back then there were still people who believed in their existence. In our existence, I should say. My mother was one of the last of them, I suppose. No one believes in us now.'

'Of course they don't,' said Tess. 'I mean, fairies! How could anyone believe in them?'

Declan plumped up a few more cushions and stretched himself out comfortably, propping his chin on his elbow. 'I think,' he said, 'that we'll have to start at the beginning. In ancient times. Do you want to explain it, Orla?'

Orla nodded and took up the story. 'I'm sure that there's nothing you don't know already,' she said. 'But maybe you forgot. Everyone does.'

'I didn't,' said Kevin.

Tess kicked him playfully. 'Smarty-pants,' she said. 'You didn't even go to school!'

'That's why I remember it,' said Kevin. 'I read it because I wanted to and not because I had to.'

'All right, all right,' said Tess. 'Go on, Orla, will you?'

She did. 'Do you remember all that legendary stuff about the *Fir Bolgs* who were the first inhabitants of Ireland, and then the *Tuatha de Danaan* came along,

Danu's people, from across the seas, from *Tír na nÓg*?'

'The Land of Eternal Youth,' said Tess.

'That's right. There are lots of stories about those people,' Orla went on. 'The books are full of them. They were a race of magicians and they could change their shape and work magic spells.'

'Oh, yes,' said Tess. 'Like the Children of Lir.'

'But do you remember what happened to them? To Danu's people?'

'I do,' said Kevin. 'There was a great battle when the Milesians came to Ireland. The Tuatha lost. They were allowed to stay in Ireland on one condition.'

Tess's skin crawled. 'I remember that bit,' she said. 'The condition was that they stay below the ground.'

There was a pause as she allowed the new implications of the old story to sink home.

'So they did,' said Declan. 'Most of the time, at least. But sometimes at night they came out and danced in the ruins of their old homes, and the rings came to be known as fairy forts.'

'And sometimes people caught glimpses of them by day as well,' said Orla. 'In wild places, like this one, where people rarely come.'

'The country people saw them often enough to know that they still existed,' said Declan. 'Even the Church failed to wipe out belief in them, though the priests tried hard enough. But a strange thing happened over the generations.'

'What happened?' asked Tess.

'We diminished in size,' said Declan.

'How?'

Declan readjusted himself again. 'It wasn't exactly that we got smaller,' he said. 'It was that people believed that we did. It's a feature of fairy glamour that we exist as people perceive us to exist. So if people expected to see "Big People", then that's what they saw. And as we became known as "Little People", then people saw us as little.'

'Anything to oblige,' said Kevin.

'Maybe,' said Declan. 'But in any event, as people's belief in us diminished, so did we.'

'But why do you keep saying "we"?' asked Tess.

'Because all of us here have *Danaan* blood in our veins. That's why we have the powers that we have.' He glanced at Kevin. 'Or had, as the case may be. For myself, I chose to keep them.'

'You were going to explain that,' said Tess. 'This is where we started from.'

'I'm getting there,' said Declan. 'When our fifteenth birthday came around, I decided to stay as I was. One of the *Tuatha de Danaan*.'

'A fairy,' said Kevin.

'If you like,' said Declan.

'And Daddy didn't,' said Orla.

'He promised he would,' said Declan, and a tone of bitterness entered his voice. 'But when it came to it he lost his nerve. He didn't believe strongly enough.'

It was like getting to the end of a jigsaw. Everything was coming together, now.

'That's why he kept visiting the woods after you disappeared,' said Tess. 'Of course everyone thought he was mad. He couldn't tell anyone the truth.'

'And that's why he wants to sell the land,' said Brian, who had run out of patience with the *Star Wars* game and come over to join them. 'And why he's so angry all the time. It still hurts him to know that Declan is here.'

Declan nodded. 'He feels that I abandoned him,' he said. 'But it was him who chickened out.'

There was a great depth of sadness in his tone as he spoke, and Tess realised that the same sense of loss was in Uncle Maurice as well, beneath the anger that arose so readily. She remembered hearing about twins; about how close they could be, and she was aware that there was something unresolved in the story.

'And now you're getting your own back, is that it?' she asked.

Declan's face revealed the bitterness he felt. 'He wants to sell the land, don't you understand? He wants to destroy my home; the only thing I have.'

'And what would happen if he did?' asked Kevin. 'Where would you go?'

'Where the rest of us go who have been displaced by what you call "development",' said Declan. 'Away from your world forever. Back to *Tír na nÓg*.'

At last Tess felt that she understood. Uncle Maurice, perpetually tormented by loss and guilt, intended to get rid of the problem once and for all, in the only way he could.

'He thought he could be free of me,' said Declan. 'But I have outwitted him.' He turned to Kevin and laughed, a sound made sinister by the words that followed. 'It was your pied piper antics that gave me the idea,' he said. 'He'll never, ever sell the place now.'

# CHAPTER EIGHTEEN

While they were talking, Colm had resumed his efforts to get out of the crawl-hole. Each time he failed he retreated and tried a different shape: a beetle, a snake, a mouse. But as soon as he got anywhere near the entrance he turned back into the porker and got stymied again.

While she watched him, Tess reflected on what she had learnt. It seemed that Lizzie was right yet again, and that it was ancestors and not ghosts that haunted the woods and wild places of the land. It made sense, too. There were plenty of stories about affairs and marriages between members of the fairy host and humans. Why shouldn't a bit of the old, wild blood have survived to enable children to use the ancient, magical power?

Colm retreated once again, and the puzzled expression on his face would have made Tess laugh if the situation hadn't been so serious.

'You can't do this,' she said. 'You can't hold the children here for ever.'

'Who says I can't?' said Declan. 'Besides, I don't have to. As soon as they get hungry enough they'll join me at my table. Then they will belong to this world, and they'll never return to that other one, out there.'

'But that's not right, Declan,' said Kevin. 'You know it's not right. People have always been tempted by the fairy world, but there was never anything in the stories about coercion. You can't force anyone to stay here if they don't want to.'

'Why not?' said Declan. 'This is my *sidhe*. In here I am the king. I can do as I please.'

Tess feared that he was right, and that none of them would ever know freedom again. But she couldn't give up.

'Why should you keep us here, though?' she said. 'Why should you want to? Your brother is out there now. He's sure to agree to any kind of deal you want, if you offer him his children in return.'

'I made a deal with him before,' said Declan, bitterly. 'He broke his word then and I don't have any reason to believe that he won't do it again. Why should I trust him?'

'Because that's what all this is about, really,' said Kevin. 'I've just realised it. This isn't the first battle of the war, is it? It's the last one. This feud has been going on between you two since you were both fifteen.'

Declan looked away and Tess knew that Kevin was right.

'He has always denied my existence,' said Declan. 'Even though he knows the truth he refuses to believe it.'

'Then talk to him,' said Tess. 'You have to give him a chance to negotiate.'

'Why?'

'Because . . .' The answer wouldn't come to Tess. She dried up. But Kevin surprised her.

'Because he's your brother,' he said. 'He's your brother and for twenty years you have lived without him, and missed him. And because he misses you every bit as much. That's why he wants to sell the land, to forget about you, not to have you haunting him every day of his life.'

'Haunting him?' said Declan. 'What do you mean, "haunting him"?'

'I've seen you,' said Tess. 'We all have. Sitting at his windows in the shape of a cat, flying over as a raven.'

'How else do you pester him, Declan?' asked Kevin. 'As a wild goat, perhaps? As a hare?'

Declan opened his mouth to speak, but what came out was more like a howl.

'He betrayed me! My whole world. He left me here alone and took over the farm. He might as well have murdered me!'

'No!' Orla had been listening quietly, but she couldn't contain herself any longer. 'Daddy wouldn't do that. He loves you, Uncle Declan, he told us that. It's why he gets so angry all the time. He's only half alive without you!'

And for all his power, for all his wealth beneath the hill, it was suddenly clear that Declan felt the same.

Tess agreed to go with Declan to be an observer in his talks with Maurice while Kevin and the others stayed behind in the *sidhe*. Declan went ahead and dived into the low tunnel as a hare. Tess followed. But as soon as they emerged into the second hall-way, Declan stopped. He was staring at the exit which, Tess could see, was wide open. On the other side of it, Uncle Maurice was standing in the moon-light, head in hands.

Tess froze, but Declan Switched back into his boy-like form. After a moment, Tess joined him.

'It's hard to believe that he can't see us,' she whispered.

'Could you see into the rock, from out there?' said Declan.

'No. But I can see out, now.'

'It's different from this side. It doesn't matter what we do, he can't see in.'

To demonstrate his point, Declan skipped along the hall and did an energetic jig just feet from where his brother was standing. Tess watched, breathlessly. Declan was a strong and graceful dancer, as skilled as anyone she had seen in any of the Irish dancing shows that had recently become so popular. He grinned at her and winked, then turned and made insulting gestures at his brother.

But Uncle Maurice might as well have been blind for all the notice he took.

'Why?' asked Tess. 'Why can't he see or hear us?'

'Glamour,' said Declan. 'There aren't so many *sidhes* like this left now, but once they were all over Ireland. We hid them; not with any actual thing, but with illusion. The door exists only in his mind, as it existed in yours before you succeeded in breaching it.'

'But if he was a Switcher himself, why doesn't he know that?'

'Because he doesn't believe any more. He has denied the past as well as the present.'

As Tess watched, Uncle Maurice struck at the invisible barrier, first with one fist and then the other. From her perspective, it looked as though he was hitting unbreakable glass.

'Are all the doors the same?' she asked.

'They work on the same principle, yes. But some are grassy hill-sides and some are in the ground. Wherever they are, they work in the same way; by deceiving the mind of the onlooker.'

At that moment, Uncle Maurice sighed loudly and turned away from the door. Without pausing for an instant, Declan transformed himself into a barn owl and, with a shrill shriek of alarm, went bursting out of the opening.

More quietly, Tess followed. As she swept up through the trees and joined Declan circling above them, she could see her uncle on the ground below, shaking his fist after them. She was glad that he couldn't see little Colm's predicament inside the hill. Angry as he was now, that would have made him mad with fury.

Still in owl-form, Declan circled above the trees and Tess followed while Uncle Maurice watched on helplessly. Not until he got tired of craning his neck and sat down despondently on a mossy rock, did Declan alight. For a while he sat in a tree, looking down, while Tess waited on a nearby branch. Then, as though he had finally plucked up courage, he dropped on to the ground below and Switched. Choosing her spot carefully, Tess glided down from the trees and Switched behind a broad trunk, from where she could look on unseen by either of the others.

In the moonlit clearing, Declan's clothes had a quite different appearance. Without colour their sheen was silvery-grey, so similar to the surrounding light that it was not easy to see him at all. Except that, when he moved in a certain way, a gleam of bluish light would suddenly shine out for an instant, then vanish again, reminding Tess of the mysterious flickerings that she had seen from her bedroom window.

It was some time before Uncle Maurice became aware of his brother's presence. When he did, his jaw dropped. Seeing them together, Tess realised why it was that Declan had seemed familiar to her when she had first set eyes upon him. The family resemblance was quite remarkable; the two boys must have been stunningly similar when they were the same age.

When they were the same age. How could they have once been the same age and be the same age no longer? Tess was trying to get her mind around the paradox when Uncle Maurice spoke.

'It really was you, then, all along?' he said. 'The raven and the cat and the brown hare. I was never sure.'

'It was me,' said Declan.

'Sometimes I thought there was nothing there at all,' said Maurice. 'Nothing except a figment of my imagination.'

He fell silent, but crossed the clearing slowly until he was close to his brother. There was no difference in their height, but one was a boy and the other a man. For a long time neither of them spoke, and Tess felt embarrassed, a stranger eavesdropping on a highly emotional reunion. Then Uncle Maurice spoke again.

'I still can't believe that it's true,' he said. 'I'm so

used to mistrusting my own senses. Everything was so confused at the time when you . . . when you disappeared. If I tried to explain what had happened, people thought I was mad.'

'People believe what it suits them to believe,' said Declan. 'Sometimes when tourists come wandering around I go and stand right in front of them and they don't see me at all.'

'That's what I'm afraid of,' said Maurice. 'Sometimes I think that you must have died, and that I created the whole story in my imagination to save me from having to face the truth.'

Declan thought for a moment. 'I've forgotten,' he said. 'I have forgotten how it feels to have a mind that needs to discover truth, instead of one that creates it.'

Maurice nodded. 'I've forgotten the other kind,' he said. 'Or at least, I stopped believing in it.'

'Why did it matter to you, then?' said Declan. 'Why did you feel the need to sell off the land and get rid of me?'

Uncle Maurice shook his head, and Tess realised that there was something he was withholding.

'Why, Mossy?' Declan pressed him. 'Why couldn't you just let it be?'

'I could have, possibly. If you had let me. But you wouldn't, would you? You had to keep haunting me. You were always on my mind, Dec. I haven't known a moment's peace since you . . .'

'Since I what, Maurice? What is your version of the truth? Since I disappeared? Since I went through with it? Or since you chickened out on our agreement?'

'Is that what you think?' said Maurice. 'All these years, you thought that I didn't have the courage?'

He shook his head. 'It wasn't like that. It was just the opposite.'

'Oh, yes?'

'Yes. Until that moment it had all been a game, like all the other "what if" sorts of game. But when you made the change, when I saw you become one of *them*, then it wasn't a game any longer. It was for real. And then I knew that I couldn't do it. Because one of us had to stay with our mother and father, Dec. If we had both vanished for ever it would have killed them.'

Behind the trunk of the tree, Tess could understand all too well how Uncle Maurice must have felt. Her parents had always been a concern of hers, whenever she thought about her future life.

'So you took the decision, there and then, is that it?' said Declan. 'Without asking for my opinion?'

'I hesitated,' said Maurice. 'I hesitated and then it was too late. The moment had gone and the sun rose. I had missed my chance.'

'You hesitated and I was lost,' said Declan.

'But you're not lost, Decco. Don't you see? At that moment, at the moment when the sun rose, I became fifteen. A fifteen year old boy, destined to become a man and a father, and then grow old and die. But you . . . You, Dec . . .'

Maurice's words tailed off as emotion choked him.

Declan looked long and hard at his brother, and something seemed to give; some hardness in him seemed to melt away and allow space for understanding to enter.

With a massive effort, Maurice succeeded in gaining control of his emotions. 'It never occurred to me before now that you should feel aggrieved,' he said. 'As far as I was concerned, I was the one who had been left behind. Stuck in a black and white world, while you're out there in the colourful one.' He paused, and then, before his sorrow could silence him again, he continued, 'For ever, Dec. For ever.'

For a long moment, the two brothers stared at each other, and then, quite suddenly, the resentment that had stood like plate armour between them for twenty years dropped away.

'I'm sorry,' said Declan. 'I never thought of those things. I never saw it like that.'

'You're not as sorry as I am,' said Maurice.

The two brothers contemplated each other for a few moments, then Maurice said, 'Are you solid? Can I touch you?'

Declan stepped forward and held out his hand. Maurice took it, held it, then pulled his brother close and hugged him tight. When he released him and stepped back, Tess could see a new light in her uncle's eyes, as though years of bitterness had dissolved away, revealing him as he had been; youthful and hopeful and kind.

'I'll let the children go, Mossy,' said Declan. 'Will you keep the land?'

'You have my word on it,' said Maurice. 'As long as I live, I'll never sell it, nor touch it in any way at all.'

'If I trust you on that, will you trust me?' said Declan. 'Will you let the children visit me?'

Uncle Maurice laughed, a new kind of laugh that Tess had never heard him make before, light and exuberant.

'I will of course,' he said. 'And I'll come myself as well. Picnics with the fairies. You can be sure of it!'

The two brothers embraced again, then broke apart and shook hands. Then Declan took two steps backwards and melted away in the moonlight.

# CHAPTER NINETEEN

Tess scanned the surroundings, trying to get a fix on where Declan had gone. But apart from a fresh breeze that was swishing around in the treetops, there seemed to be nothing moving. Uncle Maurice sat himself down to wait for the children and, after another minute or two, Tess returned to the *sidhe*.

Now that her mind had dispelled the illusion that hid the door in the rock, Tess had no difficulty passing through. Inside, she found that the easiest way to negotiate the dim hall was as a bat, and she was still in that form when she whisked through the crawl-hole. The moment she entered the second hall her hearing and her sonar perception were both assaulted by chaos.

She needed eyes. As quickly as she could she Switched into human form and tried to make sense of what she was seeing. In the middle of the hall an enormous bear was throwing its weight around in what seemed like a terrible rage. Beside it, C3PO was trying to calm it in a terribly British sort of voice, while a jackdaw fluttered around its face in a way that was clearly intended to distract it. A few feet away, Kevin was in the process of overturning the table, and the piles of food were crashing to the floor.

'Help, Tess,' he shouted. 'He's gone berserk!'

At last she realised what was happening. Little Colm had finally had enough of being thwarted. His hunger and frustration had become bear-sized, and so had he. It was a frightening situation, but Tess didn't realise just how dangerous it was until she saw what was in the bear's paws. He had succeeded in reaching the table before Kevin overturned it, and he was clutching a bear-sized fistful of sausages. The only thing preventing him from getting them into his bear-sized mouth was the persistent irritation of the jackdaw, which was in grave danger of being swiped by a flailing paw.

There wasn't a second to lose. Tess allowed her instinct to guide her as she Switched, and was surprised to find herself in the shape of a wolfhound. She was already springing forward as she took on the form, and an instant later her jaws clamped tightly around the bear's forearm. But she had underestimated Colm's power. With a bellow of rage, he swung the arm in a great arc, crashing her into Kevin and knocking him over before sending her hurtling through the air to the other end of the hall. It all seemed to happen infinitely slowly. Even as she was hitting the wall and struggling to her feet she was watching what was happening in the fray. The bear knocked the flapping jackdaw aside. His paw, with sausages sticking out like fingers, approached his mouth. And then, when it seemed impossible for anything to stop the terrible progress of fate, the bear turned into a tree.

For a moment, Tess thought that the collision with the wall had jellified her brain. From the expression on Kevin's face as he scrambled to his feet, he was having similar thoughts. But beyond him, just inside the crawl-hole, Declan's smug expression revealed the solution.

'How did you do that?' asked Tess, testing out her bruised limbs as she walked towards him.

'I'll show you,' he replied. 'As soon as I have sent this lot home.'

Orla and Brian had returned to their own forms, and if they were surprised by what had happened, they didn't show it. But Kevin was shaking his head in disbelief.

'I see what you mean,' he said. 'About the rules changing.'

Declan was picking sausages out from among the branches of the tree and eating them. 'He'll have to be careful, this one,' he said. 'He doesn't know his own strength.'

'He just gets hungry,' said Orla. 'He's good at home and at playschool. He understands.'

Declan nodded and, as soon as all the sausages were safely out of the way, he turned Colm back into a small and tearful human being.

'Don't worry now,' he told him. 'Your daddy's outside. You're going home.'

Colm did a red-booted dance of delight at the news, and Brian hefted him up on to his hip and hugged him. But Orla's face fell.

'Is he cross?' she said.

Until that moment Tess had completely forgotten about Orla's asthma. It was only now that she realised there hadn't been the slightest hint of a wheeze in her cousin's breath the whole time they had been inside the hill.

Declan was shaking his golden head. 'He's not cross at all,' he said. 'In fact, I wouldn't be surprised if he wasn't half so cross now as he used to be.'

Colm wriggled to be put down and headed for the crawl-hole. But at the point where he had become accustomed to turning into a pig he stopped and looked over at Declan.

'Go home, now?' he said.

Declan nodded. 'Go home, now,' he said.

And Colm was a red fox, scooting out through the small space as though a pack of hounds was on his tail.

'Me too,' said Brian, and was gone. But Orla hesitated.

'Will you be back soon, Tess?' she asked.

'I . . . I don't know,' said Tess. The question had brought back the terrible question of choice, and Tess knew that the ordeal of that night was very far from being over.

'I know it's your birthday,' said Orla. 'Maybe you'll come back and visit us anyway. Whatever you decide?'

Tess was surprised to discover a new respect for her young cousin. Maybe it was the illness that had caused it; the continual struggle for breath and for life, but the girl seemed wise beyond her years.

'I will, of course,' said Tess. 'Even if . . .'

Orla nodded. 'Even if,' she said. And then she was gone.

'How did you do that?' Kevin asked Declan.

Declan shrugged. 'Desperate circumstances call for desperate measures. Like a sausage?'

'Thanks.' Kevin took it and was about to put it into his mouth when Tess realised what he was doing.

'Watch what you're doing,' she yelled.

Kevin dropped the sausage, an expression of horror on his face. 'You tried to trick me,' he said.

Declan shrugged. 'Why shouldn't I? That's what I am, it's what I do.'

Tess expected to feel as horrified as Kevin, but part of her was beginning to be enchanted by Declan. His abilities seemed limitless; his power excited her. Not only that, but in comparison with Kevin's awkward, gawky frame, Declan was graceful and handsome.

'You said you'd show me,' she said. 'How to Switch other people.'

'I will,' said Declan. 'I'll show you more than that as well, if you come with me.'

'Where?'

Declan nodded towards the crawl-hole. 'Out there. To where the night is waiting for us.'

'Careful, Tess,' said Kevin.

'You could come with us, too,' said Declan. 'If you eat fairy food you become fairy, Kevin. You could be what you once were; experience your old powers again, keep them forever.'

Tess could tell that Kevin was interested. 'Why not, Kevin?' she said.

He shook his head. 'There has to be a catch,' he said. 'I'm not sure that I want to stay here forever.'

'You could be a rat again,' said Tess.

'A rat?' said Declan. 'Is that what you like best? A rat?'

Kevin looked sulky and didn't answer.

'I could sort that out for you if you wanted,' said Declan. 'Turn you into one for good. Would you like that?'

Kevin shrugged, but Tess knew that he was tempted.

'You don't have to decide right now,' said Declan. 'Have a think about it while we're gone.'

And before either Kevin or Tess could answer, Declan had become a hare again and vanished out of the crawl-hole.

'Don't go, Tess. What if he tricks you?'

'He won't,' said Tess. 'I'll be OK.'

Kevin nodded wistfully. 'You're your own boss,' he said. 'But promise me one thing?'

'What's that?' asked Tess.

'Promise me that you'll come back before dawn. Before you make your final decision.'

Tess nodded, sobered by the reminder of the short time remaining to her.

'I promise,' she said.


From the skies high above the woods, Tess and Declan could see Uncle Maurice and the others walking across the fields towards home. The grass was covered with dew and the three who were walking left straggly trails behind them as though they were in no hurry. The fourth one, little Colm, was already fast asleep, secure in his father's arms.

Beside her in the high air, Tess could sense Declan's sadness, despite the disdainful look in his eagle's eye. Somehow she knew that it wasn't only his brother he missed, but the other things as well; the life he would never lead as a farmer, the children he was unlikely to have. As though he sensed her intuition intruding upon him, he banked on the wind and drifted down to a nearby field, where cattle lay sleeping in the grass.

'Go on,' said Declan, when they had taken on human shapes again. 'Turn them into pigs first. It's good practice.'

'But how?' said Tess.

'Why ask me?' said Declan. 'How do you Switch?'

Tess knew what he meant. Although Tess could Switch as quick as thinking, there was no way she could have explained to someone how she did it. It was one of those things like wiggling your ears; you could do it or you couldn't. And when she thought about it like that, she realised that she did know how to change the shapes of other things as well; she had just never realised that she could.

The cows didn't know what hit them. One moment they were happily sleeping and the next, one after another, they were all turned into pigs. Tess laughed delightedly, and then the pigs were sheep, bleating anxiously and gathering themselves into a defensive group. But Tess wasn't finished yet. In fact, she was just beginning to get the hang of it. It was the same process as Switching; the combined use of will and imagination, and she was already regretting all the lost opportunities.

The sheep became goats, and then half of them became kangaroos. Then, while they were still staring at each other in astonishment, some of them became hyenas and began stalking the others.

'Careful,' Declan warned. 'We don't want to cause any damage.'

He was right. Things were beginning to get out of control as goats and kangaroos began to panic and spring out over the walls and away. Before they got too far, Tess Switched them all back into cows again, which is how the farmer would find them the next morning; scattered around in different fields with no evidence to show how they had got there.

'I can't believe I never discovered this before!' said Tess, turning a rock into a tractor and a field full of round bales into an igloo village. 'I could have had a great time! I can just see it, too. All those times my dad drove me mad reading the paper, I could have turned him into a sloth or a slug or a tortoise or something. And my mum, droning on. A queen bee!'

Declan came along behind, returning Tess's transformations to their original selves.

'There's a girl at school always copying what everyone else says,' Tess went on. 'I'd love to turn her into a parrot.' As she spoke, Tess changed a hawthorn bush into a Japanese pagoda and a steel gate into a large patchwork quilt. 'And there's a boy who's really horrible to his poor little dog. I'd turn him into a toad and let the dog eat him!'

With Tess Switching everything in sight and Declan changing everything back again, they made their way across the fields until they had come to the road, a half mile or so from the farmhouse.

'Haven't you had enough, yet?' Declan asked. 'There's other things I want to show you before daybreak.'

'Daybreak,' said Tess. 'Oh, my God. I keep forgetting.'

'There's still plenty of time,' said Declan. 'But I want you to meet the others.'

'The others?'

'Of course. You don't think we're the only ones, do you?'

As a last trick, Tess turned a thoroughbred brood mare into a donkey and, just for the hell of it, Declan left it as it was. Then the two friends made owls of themselves again and lifted into the darkness.

# CHAPTER TWENTY

Declan rode an upcurrent towards the top of the crag, where he landed and Switched to his golden, fairy form. Tess followed and became human. Side by side they sat for a while and watched the moon slipping down towards the horizon, then Declan turned to Tess and said, 'Want to try the weather?'

Without waiting for a reply, he stood up and held out his arms like a conductor in front of an orchestra. Tess stayed where she was. She thought it was a joke. Even when the first clouds began to appear from beneath the setting moon and creep across its face, she put it down to coincidence. But a moment later she had to reconsider.

Like a speeded-up film the white clouds advanced, obscuring the moon and rapidly covering the sky. The night became darker, and Tess dimly remembered something about the darkest hour being just before the dawn. But it didn't stay dark for long. First, a few faint pulses of light began to bounce around among the clouds. Gradually they grew stronger and more brilliant until suddenly a streak of lightning leapt from the clouds and struck the ground nearby. There was a cracking sound that could only have been made by a rock splitting.

'Woah, woah,' Tess shouted. 'Steady on, now!'

But her words were swallowed by a mind-numbing boom of thunder right above her head. She ducked instinctively and turned to suggest to Declan that they get out of there. It was clear, however, that he had no intention of moving.

The expression on his face was ecstatic, as though the chaos that he was creating in the skies around was divine music. He turned to her and smiled a brilliant smile. Again a bolt of lightning struck nearby, and then another and another, but Tess no longer feared that they would harm her. There was a smell of burning vegetation, but when she looked down towards the woods at the foot of the crag below them there was no sign of fire.

It seemed indeed that the lightning storm was confined to the top of the mountain. Tess wondered whether anyone was awake at that hour and watching. It must have been a spectacular sight. And no more extraordinary, she mused, than a lot of unexplained things that happened in human life.

The rain began, bucketing down out of the firework skies. Declan whooped and turned his face up to the downpour. And when she stopped resisting, Tess began to enjoy it as well. So heavy was the deluge that in no time at all the top of the mountain was awash with run-off, and small streams began to develop and join together to make larger ones, which

raced for the edge of the crag and launched themselves over.

Suddenly, remembering Lizzie's words, Tess knew
that wild blood did indeed run in her veins. With
careless delight, she Switched into a salmon and
flipped and flopped herself into the nearest stream.
The water lifted her and rushed her towards the edge
until, with heart-stopping speed, it catapulted her out
over the edge of the crag.

She turned in the air; head over tail in empty space.
As she fell she knew the delirium of recklessness, of
trust in her own power, of the thrill of the moment.
Below her the trees were emerging out of the darkness. Any moment now and she would smash into
their branches, become fish-cakes, a surprise delicacy
for the rats. In the nick of time she spread eagle wings
and soared away, every feather vibrating in the rain-
filled air. Out and away she swung, while above her
the downpour ended and the clouds quietened and
rolled away and dispersed, like a flock of sheep
released from a pen.

The moon reappeared, sinking behind the horizon.
For a few minutes Tess drifted, enjoying the sense of
freedom and grace that the massive wings gave her.
Then she flapped lazily upwards until she reached
Declan's side again.

Back in human form, Tess was so wet that tiny
streams dribbled from her hair and from her cuffs,
but the excitement still ran so high that she didn't
care at all.

'What next?' she asked.

'You have to learn to ride,' said Declan.

'Horses?' Tess was reminded of the unfortunate
brood mare and hoped that her owner liked donkeys.
He would probably think that a neighbour, or

someone who bore him a grudge, had changed the animals over for the mischief of it. The more she thought about it the more Tess realised that life was full of inexplicable happenings. And in their insistence on concocting 'logical' explanations, people tried to force their world into the confines of a set of laws that made it seem much smaller and less interesting than it really was.

Even when it clearly didn't fit. For now a wind was rising in the west. But this wind was not caused by changing pressures in the earth's atmosphere. This wind was Declan's, and it was summoned by a combination of will and imagination which, the old people knew, was called magic.

Declan's wind was warm and brisk. Tess wrung out her hair and her sleeves and spread out her arms to dry. But there was no time for that. Under Declan's silent command the wind began to twist and turn and, like some restless animal, it brushed against Tess and knocked her off balance. She sat on a rock and watched as Declan sent it whipping across farmland, swirling through the trees below, and howling above and between the surrounding hills. Then he brought it back where it waited at his feet with a strange quivering that made Tess's eardrums vibrate.

'You want to try?' he asked.

'OK.' Tess stood up again and took hold of an imaginary pair of reins. But it was not as simple as it had looked when Declan did it. At her first command the wind lunged away so powerfully that Tess was almost dragged over the edge of the cliff and Declan had to come to her rescue. More delicately, she tried again until, gradually, the wind began to respond to her wishes. She circled it first, like a horse on a lunge rein, round and round the flat mountain-top. Then, when she was confident with that, she sent it blustering off to the sea, so that it returned damp and salty and sounding of gulls. And then, just as she was beginning to feel confident, Declan said, 'Are you ready to ride it?'

Before Tess could reply, he rushed forward and disappeared over the edge of the crag. Tess's heart stopped, but he was only gone for a moment. When he reappeared he was astride the invisible wind, tossing backwards and forwards on its restless force as he waited for her.

'Come on, Tess!' he called.

Throughout her life, there had always been steps Tess was afraid to take. She realised now as she looked out over the immense drop below that there would never come a time, no matter what she decided to be, when there would not be another step that required courage, and then another. But there would never be another night like tonight, when there was so much to learn in so little time.

The knowledge that she could save herself by Switching gave her courage. She called up her wind and, at the same time, launched herself out over the edge.

And fell. Down, down towards the trees below. In a panic she grabbed at imaginary reins and yanked hard. Instantly, her descent began to slow.

'Up!' she yelled.

And up she went, rising with swift and certain power until she passed Declan on a level with the crag.

'East!' he shouted.

Tess banked as though she was riding a motor bike, and beneath her the wind responded. Left and right she leant. Left and right the wind turned. Declan was lost in the night ahead, but suddenly his clothes gave off a blue, moonlight gleam, and Tess sped off in pursuit. As she caught up, the two breezes buffeted around each other and gave their passengers a bumpy ride, but after a while they settled. Side by side, Tess and Declan raced through the night sky.

Not since she and Kevin had been dragons had Tess experienced such a sense of exhilaration. Beneath them the country was laid out like a map, but not a map of towns and roads and rivers. What they were seeing was a fairy map, made up of ley-lines and *sidhes* and the strongly radiating focal points of magical power.

'Scenic route,' said Declan, indicating the glowing shapes of Tara and New Grange far below. They veered north and, in a surprisingly short time, over-flew the prehistoric site of Eamhain Macha.

'Where are we going?' asked Tess.

'The gathering,' said Declan. 'I just thought you'd like a little look around on the way.'

'What gathering?' asked Tess.

Declan didn't reply but turned towards the west again, and soon they were dropping down to an area where it seemed that dozens of lines of energy came together and caused a warm, inviting radiance.

'It's Ben Bulben,' said Tess, as the unmistakable profile of the Sligo mountain revealed itself in the moonlight.

Long before they landed on its broad back, Tess could see the fairy hordes gathered there.

'Many of the *sidhes* have been desecrated,' said Declan. 'But there are still a great many undiscovered. This has always been a favourite place of our people.'

Tess hung back, intimidated by the numbers that were gathered below.

'Come on,' said Declan. 'You won't feel a bit shy when you get there. Believe me!'

# CHAPTER TWENTY-ONE

And he was right. Any shyness that Tess might have experienced evaporated as soon as she arrived. That night, on Ben Bulben, Tess moved among the people of Danu who come from the Land of Eternal Youth. She danced as she had never danced before, even in her imagination. For the first time in her life, she was home.

Crowds of them were there, the eternally young, all glowing with the soft, vibrant energy that was a property of *Tír na nÓg*. They welcomed her with ceremonial gifts; a torque of heavy gold that fitted around her neck; a ring of the same material, broad and bright. The women were beautiful and the men were handsome, but none was more handsome that night than Declan, and it was with him that Tess chose to dance.

On top of Ben Bulben and under it the party went on, and if people can never reveal or remember their visits to fairyland it is because the people and the places are not of this world and cannot be described in its terms. Lizzie's words, remembered there, were not in the slightest bit puzzling, and Tess passed on her regards to the people of *Tír na nÓg*. For these people were, she realised, her ancestors. These were the immortal ones who still lived on beneath the green fields of Ireland and would live on there as long as there were wild and unpopulated places for them to inhabit. They were older even than the ancient mountain beneath their feet, and would remain long after it had been swallowed by the sea.

On top of Ben Bulben and under it, Tess discovered what it meant to have wild blood running through her veins, and she celebrated it with reckless delight. She danced without stopping and Declan danced with her until, like a discord, a different light began to appear in the sky.

Tess stopped and, reluctantly, Declan did too. Around them the dancers whirled on and away, and vanished into the night as though they had never been.

'Dawn,' said Tess.

'Not yet,' said Declan. 'But it's coming.'

'We must go back. Quickly!'

'But why? Now that you know what you are, you need never go back there again.'

'But I have to,' said Tess. 'I promised Kevin that I would.'

Declan opened his mouth to protest but, with an authority that surprised her, Tess summoned a wind and commanded it to carry her back to the *sidhe* in the crag.

Kevin was waiting outside the door in the rock. As Tess made her dramatic arrival, he jumped to his feet.

'Thank God,' he said. 'I thought you weren't going to make it.'

'Don't worry,' said Declan, who had swept in behind her in the trees. 'There isn't any hurry.'

'I think there is,' said Kevin. 'I think that any moment now the sun is going to rise.'

'So what if it does?' said Declan. 'Tess has made her decision, haven't you, Tess?'

There was a rustling and a whispering among the trees. Although she couldn't see them, Tess knew that there were others there with them, waiting to welcome her into their company. She nodded, realising that Declan was right. She had made her decision. Now that she had found her heritage, how could she renounce it?

But Kevin was adamant. 'No, Tess. No. Think again.'

'But why?' said Tess. 'You could join us if you wanted to. You can't imagine how it feels.'

'Maybe not,' said Kevin. 'But I've been doing a lot of thinking.'

'Don't think,' said Declan. 'It's a terrible weakness that people have. I thought you were set on being a rat, anyway?'

As he said the words, he pointed at Kevin and Switched him. There he was, the rat with two toes missing, so familiar to Tess from the days when she had first known him. She experienced a sense of *déja vu*, then remembered her dream and the strong sense of foreboding that had accompanied it. Something was very wrong.

Kevin spoke to her in rat. 'Girl changing rat back

into boy. Very fast! Rat turning into boy! Rat turning into boy!'

In the background another rat voice added itself to the demand and Tess realised that Cat Friend was there, watching everything that was going on.

Tess remembered her lessons with Declan and Switched Kevin back, delighted to show off her new powers. How could she possibly give them up, now that she was discovering the full extent of them?

'Changed your mind?' said Declan, as Kevin became human again.

'Yes,' said Kevin. 'I have. I want to be human, Tess, and I think you should, too.'

'Why?' said Tess. 'Give me one good reason.'

Kevin glanced towards the east, and worry was carved into his features.

'I will,' he said. 'Just hear me out, will you?'

Declan looked disdainful, but Tess nodded and Kevin went on.

'I could live a happy life as a rat. I know I could. And you could live forever as you are; young and beautiful, a magical being. But neither of us would have influence, you see?'

'Influence?' said Declan, and as he spoke a wind rose and began to bluster around in the trees above their heads. 'What would you know about influence?'

'I'm not even sure what you are, Tess,' Kevin went on. 'Are you? Remember what Declan was saying about adapting to people's perceptions? What if that's all you are? Just a figment of someone else's imagination?'

Declan's face darkened, and he took Tess's arm as though to draw her away. But she shook her head and turned back to Kevin.

'Go on,' she said.

'I don't know,' he said, rushing his words now in a desperate race against the irresistible turning of the planet. 'I don't know what you are or what he is. But I do know that if you become like him, if that's the choice you make, then you won't belong to this world any longer.'

His words unsettled Tess. The wind in the trees got rougher, more insistent. Declan gripped her arm again.

'Don't listen to him,' he said.

But Kevin was not going to be put off. 'This world, Tess. This world that we both love so much.' He tore a clump of moss from a rock and held its earthy scent to her nose. 'I came to an understanding tonight,' he went on. 'About what it meant to be a Switcher. I realised that it doesn't matter whether or not I can change my shape; not any more. What matters is that being a Switcher taught me . . . taught you as well, Tess . . . how to adapt. How to change to meet whatever situation arises, even though we might look the same from outside.'

Tess nodded. What Kevin was saying was something that she knew and believed, even though she had never succeeded in putting words on it.

'I can see my future at last,' he was saying. 'It came to me tonight as I was waiting here. I'm going to get off the streets, Tess, get some education if I need to, do whatever it takes to get into a position where I can make a difference. These woods are safe, now, they will stay as they are. But all over the world there are wild places being destroyed. I'm going to be there, Tess. I'm going to campaign, try to stop it happening, stand in front of the bulldozers if I have to.'

A few drops of rain began to fall, but despite them

the first blackbird sang a tentative phrase from a nearby branch.

'All those creatures, Tess! We know them better than anyone. Who will fight their corner if we don't, eh?'

A light touch, light as a moth, tickled Tess's ankle. Cat Friend was there again, reaching up, her whiskers twitching. The simple gesture of trust brought a charge of emotion into Tess's bones.

'We can be their ambassadors, Tess; their voice in the world. It will help the fairy people, too, if we can save the wild places!'

Declan was tugging at her again. 'Don't listen to that nonsense,' he said. 'Stay with me, Tess, and ride the wild winds at night. Look at the gold you have on you. Look at your wealth. You'll never have such power in any other life.'

The rain fell harder. A second bird began to sing and there were two small voices in the darkness. As the first ray of the rising sun found a way past the clouds and crept in among the leaves another bird voice joined them, and then another. Kevin held out his hand.

And Tess took it.

Then all hell broke loose around them as Declan unleashed the full fury of the storm. Instinctively, Tess ducked down and shrank against the flat wall of the crag. Kevin joined her, shielding his head with his arms as lightning blasted the heart out of a huge boulder just feet away.

'It's OK,' said Tess, clutching at his jacket. 'It's OK.'

Again the lightning struck, and again. High above them it hit the exposed crag once, twice, three times.

An ominous rumble began, deep inside the mountain.

Rain drenched their hair and ran down their faces. Kevin got to his feet and dragged Tess up.

'Run, Tess,' he yelled. 'The whole lot is about to come down on top of us!'

Even as he spoke there came a deafening crack from above, as though the cliff itself had split in two.

'Come on, Tess! Run!'

But Tess held her ground. She shook her head. 'No.'

'Are you mad?' Kevin was shouting now, his voice barely audible above the creaking and groaning of splintering rock and the splashing of monsoon-like rain.

'No!' Tess shouted back. 'I'm not mad. But I know that Declan won't hurt us!'

'What do you think he's doing, then?' Kevin yelled.

There was terror in his voice. To their right they heard the crash of fracturing trees as the first huge boulder hurtled down on the woods from the crag above.

But still Tess held her ground. 'He won't hurt us,' she repeated. 'None of them will.'

Another massive chunk of rock crashed into the trees. Lightning struck repeatedly nearby, making the world smell of sulphur.

'But they're trying to kill us!' said Kevin.

Tess shook her head, absurdly calm amid the raging chaos. 'They won't kill us,' she said. 'They won't hurt us at all. They're the Good People, Kevin. The Good People.'

And as though the forces of nature themselves had heard her words, the wind dropped and the storm died away and the rain continued for just long enough to extinguish the lightning-fires, then it stopped, too.

Tess and Kevin sat on the wet moss at the foot of the crag, absorbing their experiences and waiting for daylight. Gradually the birds regained their confidence and resumed their singing, and from a nook in the rock beside them, Cat Friend peeped out.

'Lightning finished, huh, huh?' she said.

'Yup, yup.'

Tess bent down to talk to her, and as she did so, something in her jeans' pocket dug into her stomach. She pulled it out. It was Orla's inhaler.

'White Cat at home in the rock, huh?' said Cat Friend.

'Yup,' said Tess. 'White Cat, raven, hare, all back inside the rock.'

Cat Friend slipped away and disappeared, and Tess felt a stab of regret, knowing that she was unlikely to see her again, or Declan either, at least in his handsomest form.

'What's that?' said Kevin, noticing the inhaler.

'It's Orla's,' said Tess. 'For her asthma. I'd better get it back to her, in case she's looking for it.'

She stood up and Kevin joined her. 'You should, I suppose,' he said. 'Although I've got a funny feeling that she won't be needing it any more.'

He slipped an arm around her shoulders and together they began to make their way through the trees. But after a few yards, Tess stopped.

'Did you hear footsteps?'

Kevin listened hard. 'I don't think so.'

Tess looked back. 'It's like a dream,' she said. 'As though it never happened at all. If you saw the rock now, would you believe that you could walk straight into it?'

Kevin shrugged. 'I think I'd have doubts, to be honest.'

He turned back to her, and as he did so he fixed his eyes on her throat and shook his head in astonishment.

'But it happened all right,' he said. 'There's your proof.'

Tess remembered the torque and reached up to take it off. In her hand was nothing but a few twists of rusty old wire, and around her finger, where the gold ring had been, was a plastic washer from a tap.

Kevin started to laugh. 'There's your gold, Tess,' he said. 'There's your glamour.'

Despite herself, Tess laughed too. At the same moment they both stopped, each of them certain that they heard another voice laughing along with them.

But no matter how hard they listened, all they could hear was silence.